SEEING THINGS

By Melvin Ward

Chapter I

A rough track, too narrow for carts and too rough for carriages, wound up the hill. Sheep used it, and occasional walkers, though there were not many of the latter because the track led nowhere but to the top of the hill and at the top of the hill there was nothing. The only reason for going there was to enjoy the view and for most people, spectacular though they all agreed the view was, it was insufficient to justify the effort of half an hour's steep uphill walking. If they climbed the slope at all, it was not very often.

Mary Calloway was one of the exceptions to this rule. She strode along the path easily, with the confident energy of youth, sure-footed and tireless. At the age of nineteen, half an hour uphill doesn't seem very daunting. She was already over half way to the summit and walked now in sunlight, the damp November mist far behind her. When she paused to look back, which she did occasionally, tendrils of mist still drifted over the lower ground. The little town of Abbot's Sutton, which had been the start of her walk, was still softened and blurred by it. Only the tower of St Oswald's church stood out clear, rising above the pale grey blanket that still filled the streets. It looked very small from this distance, the substantial grey stone mass reduced to the stature of a child's toy.

Up on the hill, the air had been cleared by a brisk south-westerly wind that wrapped Mary's skirt and coat around the calves of her legs, a hindrance to walking. It was fresh but cold and the broad, soft brim of the hat she wore flapped up and down, threatening to detach itself from the retaining pin and fly back down the path. Hats, like skirts, were a nuisance but she was so accustomed to both that she hardly noticed them. Resolutely, she turned her back on Abbot's Sutton and continued up the track. On either side of her the ground was, at this time of year, bare and almost monochrome. There was heather and some gorse growing amongst the exposed rocks, but they were mostly brown and sere. Small trees were scattered about, stark and leafless, twisted and bent into grotesque shapes by the wind that frequently swept unchecked over this exposed terrain. A few yards away, following the path, a tiny stream rippled down from a spring somewhere further up the slope, following a course it had carved laboriously out of the rock by centuries of quiet, persistent erosion. The scene wasn't exactly pretty, especially in November, but there was a wildness about it that appealed to Romantic natures.

The summit of the hill was always unexpected to those who weren't familiar with the land. One came upon it suddenly, rounding a large outcrop of grey-green lichened stone to find there was no further to climb. You were there. To the north and south of you were other hills, all similar, all part of the same undulating ridge that stretched as far as you could see, their steep slopes folding in on one another as they descended towards the miniature town at their feet. Mary rounded the stone and was surprised and disappointed to discover she was not alone. Being alone was one of the reasons she liked the place. Now, sitting on a slab of granite that could have been purpose-made as a bench and on which she often sat herself, there was a man. He had his back to her and seemed oblivious to her arrival. Mary hesitated. The man was in army uniform, something that was hardly remarkable in those days when most young men wore uniforms of one sort or another. She couldn't decide whether to turn back quietly before he noticed her or to go on and speak to him. That seemed rather a forward thing to do (her mother wouldn't approve), but she could hardly ignore him with just the two of them there in the

2

middle of a wilderness. While she dithered, something made the man turn and look over his shoulder at her. Mary gasped and put a hand to her mouth.

"Stephen! What on earth are you doing here?"

He smiled at her; a ready, amiable smile that she knew well. "Waiting for you."

"But how did you know I'd be here? No, that's the wrong question entirely. I'll go back to my first one – what are you doing here? I don't mean on top of this hill, I mean home, in England."

Instead of answering, he shifted along the stone slab and patted the surface next to him. "Come and sit down. I've warmed the stone ready for you."

Mary sat. She was glad to, her legs felt unsteady. Despite what Stephen jokingly said, the stone hadn't been warmed. The damp chill of it was obvious even through the layers of her skirt and coat. She stared at him, having trouble believing her eyes even though he was now so close. He hadn't changed at all, though it seemed an age since she had last seen him. His face was exactly the same, long and thin with a full, sensitive mouth and deep set grey eyes. The war hadn't changed him, the way it had many men of her acquaintance. His hair, cropped very short now according to army rules, was the same pale corn-colour it had always been. Only the fringe that had always fallen over his forehead was missing, a victim of the military haircut. For some reason – it may have been the crisp November light, or it may have been a heightened state of awareness in herself – everything about him stood out clearly, as if etched in metal. The roughness of the khaki serge he wore, the contrasting smooth shine of his brown leather belt, the polished brass of his buttons, the textures were all startlingly real, even the blonde bristles on his cheek where he had neglected to shave properly. Mary saw it all with a kind of crystalline clarity that took her aback. The physical reality of having him sitting next to her was momentarily overwhelming.

3

"Is my face that interesting?" He was amused.

Mary shook herself. "Sorry. I was staring, wasn't I? It's all such a surprise, your being here."

"A pleasant one, I hope."

"Of course!" She was indignant. "How could you imagine otherwise? But I still don't understand.... Are you on leave?"

"A kind of leave, you could call it."

"But they won't want you back will they? I mean, there'd be no point, now that it's all over."

"All over?" He appeared not to understand her. "What's all over?"

"The war, of course. Don't tell me you didn't know!"

"I didn't."

"Where on earth have you been? You must be the only person in England who *doesn't* know. It's impossible for anyone not to know."

"I've been... away for a while. Isolated, I suppose. Out of touch." He sounded apologetic. "While I was there in the trenches, it didn't seem as if the war would ever end, just go on and on for ever..."

"Well it didn't. It ended at eleven o'clock sharp yesterday morning. All the men are going to be coming home, and it looks as if you're the first."

"So, were there celebrations yesterday? Everyone must have been delighted."

"They certainly were! All the shops were closed – well, all except the haberdasher's, you know what Perkins is like when it comes to profit – and everyone was out on the streets." Mary laughed at the recollection. "I've never seen anything like it. A lot of people had taken a drop too much, as they say, and they were wild! The town band was out playing, and people were dancing... Young Gertie Bates – you remember Gertie, don't you? - well, Gertie danced all the way down the High Street, kicking her legs in the air with her skirts hitched up above her knees. I think she'd had a drink or two as well. Mother was scandalised. She even went and complained to Constable Evans, but he told her the laws against impropriety had been suspended for the day and if Gertie did it again tomorrow, he'd arrest her then! I think he'd taken a few drinks himself, on duty or not. You wouldn't have recognised the sleepy old town. It was marvellous!"

Her patent delight was child-like. Stephen laughed with her. "It sounds it."

"I didn't see your parents," Mary added. "But it was all so crowded, I may have missed them."

"They may have thought it all rather too vulgar," suggested Stephen equably. "You know how proper father can be."

"You would have enjoyed it, though, I know you would."

"Yes. I envy you. It's a pity I had to miss it."

"Why *did* you miss it? I still can't believe you didn't know. The whole country's been talking about nothing else for days beforehand."

"Well," said Stephen slowly, "it's a funny sort of leave I'm on..."

"They won't expect you to go back, will they?" Mary interrupted him, reverting to her earlier concern. "They can't. There wouldn't be any point, there's nobody to fight any more. You'll be able to stay here and we can be exactly like we used to be, the two of us together. That's true, isn't it?" she appealed to him.

Stephen was silent for a moment, then confirmed, "They won't expect me back."

Mary laughed again, this time with relief. "Thank Heavens for that! I can still hardly bring myself to believe you're here."

Stephen stared down the hill at the distant town without replying. Then, suddenly, he turned his head and grinned at her. "Perhaps I'm not."

"Don't be so silly!"

5

"No," he insisted. "Perhaps if you close your eyes then open them again, I won't be here."

"In that case," Mary retorted, "I certainly shan't close them."

"Go on," he urged her. "Try it. Close your eyes and count slowly to three, then open them." His lips were curled in a mischievous grin. It was an expression she knew well. He had always been fond of playing little tricks on her, illusions and legerdemain of various kinds, then challenging her to say how he performed them. She never could. It was an old game between them and the intimate familiarity of it, as if they had never parted, never been separated by war, as if everything was just the same as it had always been; that made it welcome. Reluctantly, Mary closed her eyes and counted slowly, out loud.

"One... Two... Three."

When she opened her eyes again, Stephen had vanished. She had known that would happen. It didn't worry her, not at first. It was just Stephen playing clever tricks again. She looked around but of course she couldn't see him. There would have been no joke if she could.

"I'm coming to find you," she called out.

She ran to the rock which shielded the summit, but naturally there was no one behind it. That would have been too easy. The path wound down the slope, empty and silent. Mary searched, but there was nowhere else to look. The top of the hill was exposed, the bracken too low to conceal a man. She walked about but there were no hidden ditches or crevices in the rock, nowhere for anyone to hide, nowhere he could have reached in the short time it had taken her to count. Eventually, tiring of the game and eager to see him again, she cried out, "Stephen, where are you? I give up."

Her cry carried far over the bare hillside but there was no answer.

By the time Mary returned to her home her disappointment had been relegated to second place, overwhelmed by the primary excitement at having seen Stephen again, of knowing that he was alive and well and back with her. After two years of worrying about him, of scanning newspaper reports, torn between avid curiosity and terrible trepidation, imagining him blown to pieces or terribly wounded or – the worst possibility of all – gassed, she now knew he was safe. And the war was over so he would remain safe. That was all that mattered. The silly little tricks were nothing by comparison.

She burst into the house, calling out, "Mum, Dad! You'll never guess who I've just seen!"

The house was quiet. Mary entered the drawing room to find her parents waiting for her. Her mother sat in an armchair by the window. Her father stood in the middle of the room with his feet firmly apart and his hands behind his back, as he often did. It was a stance he adopted unconsciously now, though it had once been deliberately cultivated as one he believed expressed an imposing air of authority and responsibility. Both of them looked portentously serious. Her mother had the worried look that she often wore, a look which furrowed her brow, emphasised the lines on her face and aged her prematurely.

"You'll never guess...," Mary began to repeat herself.

"Mary." Her father's voice was firm. "You can tell us later. A letter has arrived for you. I haven't opened it because it's addressed to you in person, but I believe I know what is in it." He took his hands from behind his back and Mary saw he was holding an envelope. He turned it over, staring down at it with great seriousness, then offered it to her.

"Oh no, not now. I'll read it later. First I have to tell you..."

"No. Read it now, please. It's from France." He invested the words with an ominous significance.

Mary looked at the envelope. Only the day before she would have been horrified by it, but now it held no terrors for her Now she had that certainty so few people had possessed during the years of the war.

"It doesn't matter," she said. "I've just met..."

"Read it," her father commanded sternly.

"Oh, if you insist." She took the envelope impatiently, tore it open and extracted the contents. There was a single sheet of paper bearing a short and direct handwritten message.

Dear Miss Calloway,

It is my painful duty to write this to you because, not being the next of kin, you will not have received any official notification of the fate of Private Stephen Drake. However, he requested me, as his commanding officer, to contact you personally in the event that anything should happen to him.

I am unfortunately obliged to tell you that Private Drake was killed in action on October 25th. He died of enemy shellfire during a valiant attempt to rescue a wounded comrade. I am aware that nothing I can say will be sufficient to compensate you for the loss of a loved one, but I can assure you that no soldier could have had a quicker, less painful death and that he died bravely in a humane cause.

Yours Sincerely,
Capt. Robert Kerry, KSLI.

Mary stared at the letter.

8

"It's a mistake," she said at last, "a ridiculous mistake." Her voice was trembling.

Her father shifted uncomfortably, looking down at his feet and at a loss for anything to say. He was a man out of the old English mould and did not know how to deal with strong emotions. They embarrassed him.

"Mr and Mrs Drake," her mother gently helped him out, "had the official notification yesterday, on Armistice Day. A terrible thing it must have been, to get such a letter on a day like that. We've only just found out about it. I'm afraid it's not a mistake, my dear."

"Mistakes like that," said her father gruffly, "don't happen often. I realise you must be very upset, but..."

"No!" said Mary vehemently. "That's what I was trying to tell you, but you wouldn't let me. I saw Stephen this morning, not half an hour ago."

There was a short but very profound silence.

"Perhaps it was someone else you saw, dear," said her mother at last. "Someone who looked rather like him."

"No. It's not as if I just glimpsed him from a distance or anything of that sort. I sat next to him. I talked to him. It was Stephen, he hadn't changed a bit. Do you think I wouldn't know my own fiancé?" Her parents exchanged looks. They were meaningful looks, though Mary couldn't decipher them. "Do you think I imagined it all?"

Her father stirred himself. "I'll... er, I'll contact the War Office, make sure everything's in order. Though if Stephen *is* in the area, the whole thing should sort itself out fairly quickly, don't you think? After all, you won't be the only one to have seen him. There will be his parents, his friends and so on..."

His voice tailed off into silence. They do think I imagined it, Mary realised. That's exactly what they think. Exasperated, she threw the letter on the floor and stormed out of the room.

Chapter II

The High Street of Abbot's Sutton was a steep hill, running from the railway station at the bottom to the church of St Oswald at the top. In between was a fairly prosperous-looking collection of shops and businesses. Throughout its length, various side streets branched off lined with houses, mostly terraced and built of red brick though some were older, half-timbered structures whose upper storeys leaned out over the street. These side streets were largely empty but the main road was busy with people who were either shopping, baskets over their arms, or just walking about on their own business. The traffic was mostly horse-drawn vehicles, carts and carriages, though there were a couple of motor cars and a van was parked outside a grocer's, making a delivery. There was a name painted large on the side: 'Calloway & sons, Wholesale Provisions'. The overall impression was of a quiet, self-contained community that was taking care of itself nicely, thank you very much, without much interference from outside.

Emily Duncan walked up the High Street slowly, looking around her. The place was not so small that the presence of a stranger was noticeable but even so she was conscious of curious glances following her progress. It was her appearance that attracted attention, she realised. She had a trim figure and an oval face whose features were regular if not particularly pretty, but she was not a strikingly attractive woman. She knew that and had always known it. The glances came more from women than from men and it was her clothes that gave rise to them, not her face. She wore a Burberry gabardine coat with a fur collar, appropriate for the time of year, and a domed hat with a wide brim that left room for the chignon of dark hair at the back. It was all conventional enough but it was also, for anyone who was aware of such things, very obviously expensive. Many of the women – but few of the men – were perfectly aware.

Part of the way up the street, Emily spotted a young postman going about his round on the other side. She hurried across and stopped him.

"Excuse me but I'm not familiar with the town. I've only just arrived. I'm looking for the house of a Mr and Mrs Calloway. Do you happen to know...?"

"Calloway? There's only one Calloway family here as far as I know."

"That one?" Emily indicated the delivery van.

"That's them, the same. You go up to the crossroads and turn right. It's about... ten houses or so along on your right, a big brick place called the Cedars. I don't know why it's called that, there isn't a cedar anywhere near it, but that's what it's called."

"Perhaps there used to be cedars at some point?"

"Not in my time," said the youth in a tone of finality. He couldn't have been more than about eighteen years old. "There's a nameplate on the gatepost. You can't miss it."

Emily thanked him and went on. She had little faith in the confident assertion 'you can't miss it'. Locals always said that and, in her experience, it was always possible for a stranger to miss it. That was, in fact, what happened. The road was lined on the right with houses that were very similar to one another, all apparently built to the same basic pattern and probably by the same builder at the same time, each one detached and standing in its own small garden. Any one of them could have been described as a 'big brick place'. The nameplate of the Cedars turned out to be half obscured by a thick, evergreen hedge and it was the twelfth not the tenth house along. She had passed it without noticing and had to turn back. Not too bad though, all things considered.

11

She walked along the short paved path to the front door and found a brass bell-pull with a tiny plaque underneath it saying 'Please Ring.' Dutifully, she rang and the door was answered by a maid.

"Yes, Miss? Can I help you?"

"I'd like to see Mr Calloway if he's at home, or Mrs Calloway if he isn't. They aren't expecting me."

"I can go and see if he's at home, Miss."

"Thank you. You can take him my visiting card."

The maid took the card and studied it. It was designed to impress, printed in an elegantly calligraphic script on good quality cream board. The address located her in a quite fashionable area of London. The maid looked from the card to its owner, took in the hat, the Burberry and the soft leather boots. Everything conspired to produce the intended effect.

"I'm sure Mr Calloway will see you, Miss. If you'll just wait in the hall a moment. What reason shall I give for your visit?"

"You may say it concerns his daughter Mary."

The maid disappeared. Emily waited, looking around the small, narrow hallway. It was an ordinary place, quite dark because the only light came from the door which had glass panels to its top half and small windows on either side, but all the glass was leaded and stained with a floral design. A coat rack on one wall took up space and added to the sense of constriction. The wallpaper was heavily patterned. Overall, Emily considered, it looked as if someone had made the worst of an already bad job. If rooms truly told one anything about their owners, Mr Calloway would be old-fashioned, dull and ponderously serious.

The maid returned promptly and showed Emily into a drawing room, heavily furnished in the Victorian style. Both Mr and Mrs Calloway were there, she sitting in an armchair by a window looking worried and anxious, he standing in front of the fireplace, feet apart and hands clasped behind his back. Small flames flickered amidst the coal in the fire behind him, making the modest room uncomfortably warm. As Emily had predicted, he had an old-fashioned look about him, not only in his sombre clothes but also in his square, stern features. He was a solidly-built man, not fat exactly but... corpulent. The old word suited him perfectly. His hair was receding from a low forehead and he sported bushy side-whiskers that would not have been out of place in a studio portrait from the 1850s. He was in his forties but appeared closer to sixty. A prosperous businessman, thought Emily; first generation money, self-made and hard-earned. Everything about him proclaimed it.

He cleared his throat and addressed her. "Miss... er," he consulted her card, "Miss Duncan. Please take a seat. I don't believe we've met."

"We haven't." Emily took the proffered chair and occupied it in the manner she sensed would meet with his approval: seated on the edge, knees firmly together, hands resting in her lap and elbows tucked in to her sides. She was playing a necessary role; if she did not please this man it would be difficult for her to achieve anything.

"Your business, I believe you said, concerns Mary. May I ask in what way?"

"I read the recent newspaper report relating to her fiancé..."

She got no further. Calloway flushed, his face turning the same shade of red as the bricks of his house. It was an instantaneous reaction and it did not bode well for his blood pressure. "If you have any connection with that disgraceful rag, I'll thank you to leave my house immediately."

"I don't," said Emily quickly. "Do I look like a newspaper reporter?"

"You certainly do not, my dear." It was Mrs Calloway's first contribution, delivered in a quiet, calm voice. "And we certainly saw enough of them for a few days to recognise them straight away."

"More than enough," agreed her husband curtly. However, his wife's intervention had served to quench his anger. The unhealthy flush was subsiding.

"No," Emily hurried on, "I have no connection with any newspaper, and as it happens I share your opinion of most of them. However, I am obliged to read them in the course of my work. I go through them regularly searching for stories of this kind."

"And what is your work?"

This was the awkward moment, the moment at which many people became incredulous, amused or sometimes actively hostile. She approached it cautiously. "I am a member of the Society for Psychical Research and of several similar organisations. My work, for which I am not paid in any way and which I undertake purely in a spirit of enquiry, is to investigate stories that purport to describe supernatural occurrences."

She phrased it very carefully, then paused to assess the response. To her surprise, Calloway burst into laughter. "That's a peculiar occupation for a woman, Miss Duncan. If you'll forgive me saying so, I'm not surprised nobody will pay you for it."

"Women have had many peculiar occupations over the past four years, Mr Calloway."

"That's true enough, but not many of them as odd as yours. At least making munitions has a practical value, even if it shouldn't be a job for a woman." He seemed to have softened a little, lowering his shoulders that had been braced back and relaxing his self-important stance in front of the fire. It was as if he had been tensed up against anything she may say, and now accepted her as a harmless crank. That was not an unusual reaction amongst men of his type, men who regarded themselves as down-to-earth, hard-nosed and as they would see it, realistic.

Mrs Calloway, unexpectedly, said, "It sounds to me like extremely interesting work. I visited a medium

14

myself once, after my late father passed on. It was fascinating."

"A waste of time and money," said her husband firmly. "The woman was a charlatan. You admitted as much yourself afterwards."

"Yes," said Mrs Calloway sadly. "Yes, she was as it turned out. Someone caught her out in some trickery not long after I saw her. Something to do with wires and mirrors, it was. In fact, I think it may have been someone from your organisation who exposed her, my dear. I seem to remember reading that at the time. Is that the sort of thing you do?"

"Sometimes, yes. I must admit though, that every medium I've ever encountered has been a fraud."

"They all are," affirmed Calloway. "All of them."

"But one can't know that, dear, can one?" his wife asked reasonably. "Not unless someone has investigated them."

"That's my view entirely," agreed Emily. "That's why I do it." She had found an unanticipated ally.

"So you don't believe in any of it?" Calloway challenged her.

"I don't think it should be a matter of belief. It should be a matter of evidence and proof." If her answer was evasive, Calloway didn't notice.

"Quite right." She was winning him over, with the aid of his wife. Emily caught Mrs Calloway watching her across the room with what could only be described as a slightly sly expression on her face. It occurred to her that an odd sort of game was being played, the two women manipulating the hard-headed businessman without him being aware of it. Emily revised her initial impression of the relationship between the Calloways. This, she thought, was a game Mrs Calloway had played many times before and at which she was expert.

"So," Calloway continued. "What precisely is it that you want with Mary? There are no mediums or spiritualist nonsense involved in this. It was just an

15

ordinary mistake blown out of proportion by some sensationalist newspaper hack."

"Hardly ordinary, dear," his wife demurred. "It was all quite unusual, you must admit. Personally, I would be interested to discover what Miss Duncan thinks of it all."

"Well I wouldn't. No offence intended, Miss Duncan, but I've had quite enough sordid publicity and I don't want any more. If I ever find out who released this to the newspapers in the first place..." He left the threat unfinished, possibly because he couldn't think of any convincing way to end it..

"There wouldn't be any," Emily reassured him. "None whatsoever. All I want to do is talk to your daughter, quietly and rationally, and find out exactly what she saw. In the interests of scientific enquiry of course, nothing else."

Calloway released a short laugh. "Talk quietly and rationally to Mary? I've been trying to do that for years without success."

"Now now, dear. The girl's not as silly as you make her out to be. I'll admit," Mrs Calloway added, leaning towards Emily with a confidential air, "she can become a little emotional at times, but she's still young. I'm sure she'll grow out of it."

Emily smiled at her, a smile from one conspirator to another. "One must make allowances for youth."

"That's what I always say."

"Oh, very well." Calloway capitulated with bad grace. "But I insist on being present at the interview."

"Well..." Emily tried to think of a tactful reason for objecting. Mrs Calloway saved her the trouble.

"That would never do, dear. You know perfectly well what Mary's like. If you're there, she'll refuse to say a word. Either that or she'll have one of her rebellious fits and say all sorts of ridiculous things just to annoy you."

Calloway hesitated, and was lost. "But nothing," he stipulated sternly to save face, "is to be made public. Nothing at all."

"Nothing," agreed Emily solemnly.

After an interlude while arrangements were made, Emily met Mary Calloway in a small room on the first floor of the house. It looked as though its primary use was as a dressing room but possibly it doubled as a sitting room of sorts; there were a couple of comfortably upholstered chairs and Mary was sitting on a padded chest positioned under the window. She wore a blue smock dress with a wide collar and buttons down the front, not unlike a munitions worker's overall. It was a style popular amongst girls in their teenage years. Her hair was long but pulled back into a loose bun at the nape of her neck, similar to Emily's own but less tidy. She appeared, Emily thought, younger than her nineteen years. She regarded her visitor warily with wide, unblinking eyes.

"Hello," she said.

"Hello."

"Why are you here?"

"Didn't your father explain?"

"He tried to, but I don't think he really knew either."

"I see. May I sit down?"

"Help yourself." The tone was deliberately casual, but the eyes were still wary. Emily sat in one of the chairs and took a notepad and pencil from her bag.

"Are you going to take notes of what I say?"

"Possibly. If I need to. Do you object?"

"No."

"I'm here to talk to you about what happened when you met Stephen Drake recently. I'd like you to tell me about it."

17

"I will if you want me to. I don't mind talking about it. I like your clothes," Mary added irrelevantly. "I wish I could have clothes like that. You look very elegant."

"Thank you. When you do get them you'll probably look much better in them than I do. You're prettier."

Mary smiled at that and the smile transformed her face. She really *was* a pretty young woman. "That's very honest of you." She didn't bother to argue with the assessment. She was completely and confidently aware of her own attractions. "Why do you want to talk about Stephen? You're not from a newspaper or dad would never have allowed you in."

"No, but it was the newspaper report that brought me here. I study... unusual happenings."

"There wasn't anything unusual about it. The only unusual thing is the mistake the War Office seems to have made."

"Also," Emily pointed out, "the fact that nobody else has seen Mr Drake since you did. If he really is in the area, that's rather odd isn't it?"

"Yes, it is. I can't explain it. I don't pretend to. I don't care. All I know is that I saw him and talked to him. If people won't believe me, that's their business."

"Was it you who talked to the newspapers?"

"Certainly not!" Mary sounded genuinely indignant. "Why should I?"

"Do you know who it was? Did you tell many people about it?"

"No, only the family. Then my father told the doctor and he came and examined me. He said I was probably hysterical and prescribed a powder to calm me down."

"Good heavens! And what was the effect of this powder?"

Mary studied her for a moment, then shrugged and said, "I don't know. I never took it. Elsie – she's the maid

– Elsie dissolved it in a glass of water and put it next to my bed at night. When she'd gone I tipped it out of the window." She giggled at the memory.

With some difficulty, Emily suppressed a smile. "Who else, besides the family and the doctor?"

"Only the vicar."

"Why the vicar? Did your father think an exorcism was necessary?"

Mary laughed. "Perhaps he did at that! But I didn't mind. The vicar's quite a decent old chap. We talked a bit, then he went away. He didn't seem as bothered as everybody else by what I told him. It was just a chat, that's all."

"So," Emily returned to the point, "who could have told the newspapers?"

Mary tilted her head on one side, thinking. "I believe it was George," she said eventually. "He's my brother. There are two of them, but George is the eldest. He works in the family business and he's always complaining that dad keeps him short of money. He probably thought he'd make a few pounds from the papers."

"He was probably right," said Emily.

"Do you think I should tell dad?"

"No. Definitely not."

"I expect you're right. There'd be an eruption. Dad would go purple and shout, the way he does when he gets excited. And after all, I'm not at all sure about it."

"The eruption would be fun to watch, though?"

"It would, wouldn't it?"

"Still, best not to say anything if you're not certain."

"No." Mary sounded regretful.

"So," Emily brought the conversation back to the point, "Are you going to tell me what happened?"

"If you like. It was up there." She gestured towards the window next to her. Beyond it, Emily could see the summits of the hills that dominated the town. "Stephen and I used to go up there quite often before he was conscripted. It was somewhere we could be alone together. We were going to be married before the war got in the way, did you know that?"

"I gathered it."

"There was nothing formal, but it was understood. He bought me a ring." She held out her hand, proudly displaying the ring, a gold one with a small inset diamond. "My parents didn't object – well, not much anyway – and neither did his. It was generally regarded as settled. But when he had to go into the army, we talked about it and decided to wait."

"You both decided?"

"Well, it was Stephen really. He said he wouldn't feel right about it, the fact that he might never come back and would leave me as a widow. I thought it was a bit silly, but I went along with it. I could see what he meant and he was quite firm about it. He wasn't usually very firm," she added, "but he was about that. While he was away I used to walk up there quite often, just to sit and think about him. It was comforting, somehow."

"And that was where you went on November the twelfth?"

"Yes. The day before, Armistice Day, had been special. The war was all over. Stephen could come back and we'd be able to get married at last. I wanted to sit and think about it. Then, when I got there, there he was waiting for me. It was like a miracle. I shouldn't think the vicar would approve of me saying that, but it was."

"Tell me about it. Everything you remember."

Mary did tell her, sometimes having to be prompted for details but never hesitating. Emily took notes as unobtrusively as she could, but Mary was wrapped up in her reminiscence and would probably not have noticed anyway. When she had finished, Emily laid down her pencil.

"So it was a very clear day up there? No fog or mist or anything like that?"

"No. It was gloriously clear. Everything seemed to stand out somehow. It was like one of those stereoscopic images. You know the kind I mean? The ones you need a viewer to see properly but when you have the viewer they look... even more real than reality itself."

"I know the ones. So despite what the newspapers say, it never occurred to you that what you had seen may have been a ghost or something of the sort?"

"Of course not. What I saw was Stephen. There was absolutely nothing ghost-like about him. That's a stupid idea. And," she added with a touch of childish spite, "if it *was* George who told the newspapers that idiotic story, I shall get my own back, you see if I don't."

"I'm sure you will," said Emily. "Oh, and there is one more thing. You saw Stephen, you spoke to him, but you haven't said... Did you touch him at all?"

"Certainly not." Mary reacted with indignation as if she had been accused of some immoral act.

"I mean," Emily explained, "holding hands, a peck on the cheek, that sort of thing. It would be natural enough under the circumstances."

"No, we never touched. Is that all?"

"For now, yes." Emily stood up.

"I love your coat," said Mary. "Where did you get it?"

Emily looked down at herself. "A shop in Burlington Arcade, I think. Why?"

Mary sighed heavily. "Oh, nothing."

Chapter III

It is not usually too difficult to locate a vicar. You try the church and the vicarage and if he's not in either, there will be someone who knows where he is. Emily started with the church. She had been intrigued by Mary's mention of her conversation with the vicar and thought it would be worth speaking to him, if only to compare notes. The clergy, she knew from experience, could be either valuable allies or implacable enemies to one in her occupation. It all depended on personality and theological preferences. The fact that Mary had described her local vicar as 'a decent old chap' was promising but by no means conclusive.

She had already tried the church. Despite its promisingly mediaeval dedication, it turned out to be an uninteresting building so much altered during the previous century that its original structure was indecipherable. There was nobody about, no company other than the cold, stone echoes one found in every ecclesiastical building in England. She left it without regret and stood outside the porch, looking around for the vicarage that had to be nearby. At that point, the vicar found her rather than the other way round.

"May I help you? You look a little lost." He had appeared around the side of the church while she was facing away from it and his voice made her jump. "I'm sorry, I startled you."

"I was preoccupied. As a matter of fact I was looking for you, assuming you're the vicar here."

"I am, as you can no doubt see." He held out his arms in a pantomime of display. He was wearing a full black cassock, shiny from years of use, with an old overcoat thrown over it against the cold and a thick tweed cap. He looked frankly ridiculous but undeniably clerical. Emily had been misled by Mary's casual description of him; she had forgotten that to a nineteen year-old anyone on the wrong side of forty could legitimately be described as 'old'. The vicar was a tall, gaunt man – his coat and cassock flapped loosely about his frame in the winter wind – but he could not have been more than fifty. As he spoke to her he doffed the cap politely to reveal hair that was greying and rather sparse, a feature that was emphasised by the fact that he wore it longer than was fashionable. The face was long, narrow and lined, though no more than one would expect of a man of his years, and the eyes were bright and sharp behind a pair of wire-framed spectacles.

"Then I hope you *can* help me, if you want to."

"That sounds unduly pessimistic. Why should I not want to help you? It's part of my job, after all."

"I'd like to talk to you, if you can spare the time."

"I have the rest of the day free until choir practice this evening. May I ask what you want to talk about?

"I've been to see Mary Calloway this morning and she said..."

The vicar held up a hand to cut her short. "You don't need to say any more. I can guess what it must be about, there's only one topic of conversation relating to Mary these days. We can go into the vestry if you like, or you can accompany me to the vicarage where it will be warmer, more comfortable and I may be able to tempt you with a pot of tea."

Emily smiled. "You make the choice a very easy one."

When they reached the vicarage, a large, imposing house in its own extensive garden, the vicar removed his cap and overcoat and immediately looked less eccentric and more like a traditional scholastic type of clergyman; still careless of his appearance, but that would not be out of character for such a type. The room into which he led her was also in character. It was clearly used as a study.

23

That was obvious from the bookshelves that lined the walls, filled with mostly old volumes that appeared to be in no particular order, and from a sturdy but battered old desk stacked with precarious heaps of paper the bottom layers of which could not have been moved for months if not years. A pair of architectural prints and a water-colour of local scenery hung on the walls and were the only decoration. There was nothing to hint at the vicar's vocation; it was an academic's room more than it was a clergyman's. He apologised for the mess, but the apology was a perfunctory gesture from someone who had patently ceased to notice it himself many years ago but accepted that other people may be less tolerant of it. An elderly housekeeper made an appearance and tea was requested. The vicar indicated the only concession to human comfort in the room – two winged leather armchairs with worn arms and sagging seats that looked as though he had brought them with him from his Oxford set ta quarter of a century ago.

"Please, take a seat. Not what you're used to, I'm sure, but they're really quite accommodating."

Emily sat while the vicar went to the desk and stood staring thoughtfully at a pipe rack lined with old briars.

"Do you mind?" he asked.

"Not at all."

"Oh good. I find it so much easier to relax when I have a pipe, I don't know why but it soothes the mind. Of course, when I was a young man it was considered bad form to smoke in the presence of women but things have changed since then, haven't they?"

"They have."

His hand hovered over the rack until eventually he selected a pipe. To Emily they all looked alike and the process of choosing one rather than another was completely mysterious. However, the vicar for reasons of his own seemed satisfied with his choice and began to fill the pipe from a tobacco jar next to the rack.

24

"Now, we haven't been introduced..."

Emily produced one of her elegant cards and handed it over. The vicar temporarily interrupted his pipe-filling to stare at it. "Good heavens. How impressive, Miss Duncan. I'm afraid I don't run to anything so efficient but my name is Anthony Small – vicar of the parish of St Oswald, as you know. Perhaps I should have some cards printed? But no, there would be no point. Everyone I meet already knows who I am. In my case, it would be pure affectation."

"A Doctor of Divinity, by any chance?" Emily asked.

"Why, yes. How did you know that?" Without answering, Emily ran her eyes around the book-lined room. "I see. I'm afraid most of the volumes have been unopened for many years but somehow it's comforting to be surrounded by them; enveloped by learning, as it were, even if most of it has been long forgotten. Ah, here's the tea."

The housekeeper reappeared with a tray. She poured two cups and handed one to each of them without a word. She had a plump, round face that should have been mobile but was now set like a stone mask. Emily detected an aura of disapproval at a woman like herself being invited into the vicar's study, a potential Jezebel invading the sacred precincts. Some pious and elderly widows became over-protective of their clerical charges. Emily smiled at her but the smile was deflected by a frozen glance. After she had left, the Reverend Small said, "You mustn't mind Mrs Claypole. She's a very good woman but she does tend to try to mother me. It's an occupational hazard for an unmarried vicar, I'm afraid."

"You never married?"

"On the contrary, I was very happily married for a few years; too few. My wife died in childbirth and I was never inclined to marry again."

"I'm sorry. I suppose if it was in childbirth, there was at least some compensation for your loss..."

25

"No. The child also died."

"Oh." Emily said no more. The standard platitudes seemed hopelessly inadequate. She wondered, not for the first time, how anyone's religious faith survived such manifestations of the world's casual cruelty.

"It was a long time ago. You yourself have never married?"

"Never."

The vicar nodded and made no comment. Emily was at least spared any chatter about 'the right man' or the joys of family life. The vicar spent some time lighting his pipe, disappearing temporarily behind a cloud of grey smoke. When the smoke had settled and the pipe was smouldering to his satisfaction, he sat back in his chair.

"So you have been talking to Mary Calloway. May I ask what is your interest in the matter?"

Emily launched herself into her usual account of herself, her membership of the Society for Psychical Research, her work in the investigation of supposedly supernatural occurrences. The Reverend Small watched her carefully all the time, but did not interrupt and made no comment until she had finished. She found his silent, unwavering gaze through the spectacles slightly unsettling. He was like a botanist contemplating an interesting specimen; or possibly it was the look a psychoanalyst had when presented with a new patient. Whatever it may have been, it was unlike any reception she had previously encountered and it gave absolutely no clue to the nature of his own response.

"I see," he said when she had finished. "That sounds quite fascinating. It must occupy a great deal of your time and energy."

"Yes, it does."

"And now you would like some information from me."

"Yes. I'd like to know anything you can tell me about the people involved. They are all strangers to me, but not to you. I would also like to compare what Mary told you with what she told me. Little inconsistencies can be very important in these matters."

The vicar nodded. "Yes. There is a question of confidentiality, of course. There may be things I cannot in all conscience tell you."

"If they were told to you in confidence, of course I will respect that."

"Good. Then there is only one more thing to be disposed of before we start in earnest. You are asking me to give you information. Am I allowed to ask for some information from you in return?"

"Naturally. If there is anything I can tell you, I will."

"You *can* tell me," said the vicar, "but you may not want to."

"We shall see."

"Why do you do it?" he asked abruptly. "Why do you sacrifice so much time and energy looking into things that most people would think are too ridiculous to bother with, and some would think are spiritual and therefore inherently inexplicable? What are your reasons?"

Emily answered without hesitation. "Academic interest. The spirit of scientific enquiry. A desire to resolve mysteries and expose truth to the light of day. You have been a scholar yourself; do you need more than that?"

"Yes."

"I'm sorry," said Emily firmly, "but there is no more."

The vicar took the pipe from his mouth and his lips curled in a gentle smile. "That," he said, "is untrue."

"Do you accuse me of lying?"

"Yes. Excuse my bluntness, I really intend no offence. The thing is, men in my profession are lied to surprisingly often. It is usually because people are embarrassed, or they feel guilty, or they are afraid I will judge them harshly. They have things that, for one reason

27

or another, they would rather not tell to a parson. One learns, over the years, to recognise the signs. And what you have just said to me, Miss Duncan, if you will pardon my saying so, is not true. There *is* something more."

Emily sat in silence for a while. The vicar sat opposite her, patiently smoking his pipe and waiting for her. "Very well," she admitted at last. "You're right, there is more to it than that. However, it's not something I am prepared to talk about."

"Ah, something of a personal nature. I thought so. Well, I have no desire to pry; I respect your reticence providing you can assure me that whatever it is, it will not affect your judgement."

"It won't. It never has done. I try only to establish fact and to distinguish it from deception or illusion."

"Good. Then we will say no more about it. Now, about Mary and Stephen; perhaps a little background may be in order." He leaned his head back against the chair and puffed away placidly while he collected his thoughts. The smoke curled up towards the ceiling. It was, Emily thought, an oddly sweet smell, not unlike incense, an appropriately ecclesiastical smell. "Mary you have already met and no doubt you have formed your own opinions. I find her an amiable enough young woman, a little headstrong and impulsive, inclined to be carried away by her emotions, but fundamentally quite sensible."

"Not the type to be susceptible to hallucinations?"

"In my judgement, no. To some exaggeration perhaps, or even to a degree of self-deception, but not to deliberate falsehood or invention. I believe she did see what she said she saw."

"Or at least truly believes she saw it?" suggested Emily.

"I don't know precisely what she told you, but the account she gave to me was a quite ordinary and mundane. If it had been a product of her imagination,

28

conscious or otherwise, I'm sure it would have been considerably more lurid and Romantic."

"Yes. I thought that, too. What about Stephen?"

"Oh, he was a nice enough lad, always very well-meaning and helpful. Everyone liked him. He used to sing in the choir here," the vicar added irrelevantly, "until his voice broke."

"But what you knew of him is compatible with Mary's account of her experience?"

"Oh yes. He could easily have spoken like that, behaved like that. Nothing was out of character. He was always a relaxed, easy-going type. If he had a fault, it was lack of ambition; but there are far more grievous sins than that."

"So their engagement was unobjectionable. Two pleasant young people fond of one another. I seem to remember..." She briefly consulted her notes. "Yes, she said her parents didn't object to the match, or 'not much, anyway'. Those were her words. I was curious about that. Were there any reasons for anyone to object?"

The Reverend Small sighed. "Not as far as I am concerned, and probably not as far as you are concerned either, but people have their own values and priorities. The Calloways you possibly know something about already. Mr Calloway started his working life as the owner of a little grocery shop. He worked hard and grasped opportunities when they arose. He soon had more than one shop. Then he moved into wholesale. Later, he even started importing some of his own goods. Altogether, he did very well for himself and is now a prosperous man."

"A self-made man. Yes, that's the impression he gives."

"He's enormously proud of it and has every right to be. However, the Drakes are very different; almost polar opposites, one could say. Mr Drake is a local schoolmaster, a decent man and a regular attender at church. However, I would judge that his true deities are

29

social respectability and academic achievement. He was a good father to Stephen, according to his lights, but I believe he was disappointed by the boy's lack of ambition. Stephen had intelligence enough, but lacked the drive to make the most of it. His father would very much have liked to send him to university but didn't have the means. To be honest, I doubt Stephen would have been successful anyway. He simply wasn't interested enough."

"I begin to understand," said Emily. "On the one hand we have the Calloways whose lives are built on commercial and financial success, and their daughter wants to marry the son of a poor schoolmaster. On the other hand, we have the frustrated academic whose son wants to marry the daughter of a common tradesman."

"Exactly. You have it. It all seems very dated in this day and age, but these things still matter to many people. I spoke to Mr Drake once, shortly after Stephen had been called up, and do you know what he said to me? He talked about Mr Calloway. 'He may not stand behind the counter these days', he said, 'but the man's still a grocer'." The vicar laughed ruefully. "Can you believe such attitudes persist? Still, the young pair were very attached to one another and there really wasn't any good reason for either of the families to oppose the match, even if they weren't particularly pleased with it. I imagine that was what Mary was referring to when she made that comment to you. On both sides, their engagement was tolerated rather than greeted with enthusiasm."

"And the marriage was postponed because of the war?"

"Yes, the usual reason. There is always the possibility that a soldier will leave a widow behind him, and especially if she happens to be with child... It's perfectly understandable. There would be practical and emotional hardship. Whether one agrees with it or not... well, I for one wouldn't presume to judge. People must make their own decisions on such things." The vicar took his pipe from his mouth, studied it carefully, then replaced it. Like many men, he evidently used the pipe as a means of punctuating his conversation, allowing time for thought. "So, there is the background. Does it help?"

"It may do. I don't know yet. I was wondering whether it may be profitable for me to speak to Stephen Drake's parents..."

"I would advise against trying. They are extremely distressed. The notification of his death was bad enough, especially on such a day – one of those awful official forms, a B. 104–82, can you imagine anything more soulless? 'It is my painful duty to inform you that a report has been received...' and so on. Just fill in the name and date by hand, the rest is official uniformity. Such things are atrocious." He spoke with vehement passion.

"I suppose," Emily said in a conciliatory tone, "it is a matter of the numbers involved. A truly personal notification to everyone would be impractical."

"They are not numbers, they are human beings. They deserve better than that from the country they died for. Practicality is a mere excuse for lack of compassion."

"I can't disagree with you."

"No. I'm sorry, I feel strongly about these things. But as I was saying, the Drakes are upset and this matter of the newspaper reports has made things worse. I'm afraid they blame Mary for it. The two families are no longer on speaking terms. If you approached them, not only would it increase their distress, they would be quite likely to show you the door without ceremony. As I said, I strongly advise against it."

"I'll take your advice. There's probably little they could tell me anyway. That leaves us," she glanced down at her notebook, "with Mary's story. As is often the case, there is nothing to corroborate or disprove it. We have what she says she saw, and that is all we have."

"And can you offer any explanation of her story?"

"No. There are several possibilities, of course. She may simply have made it up, but then one has to ask, why should she do such a thing?"

"Also, it is very detailed for a pure fabrication."

"It is. In addition, it is actually quite prosaic. One would imagine that if a young woman like Mary had made up a story, as we discussed earlier, it would be somewhat more conventionally supernatural."

"Indeed."

"The second possibility is that she did in fact see Stephen Drake, just as she said she did. That, however, leaves a number of unanswered questions. How was the mistake about his death made? Why has he not contacted anyone else he knew, not even his family? How did he get back to England without the army knowing anything about it? The entire hypothesis is fraught with difficulty."

"It is. And the third possibility?"

"The third possibility is that Mary did, in fact, see what one might, for want of a better word, call a ghost."

The vicar returned to fiddling, completely unnecessarily, with his pipe. In the process it went out and he had to devote time to relighting it. "And is that your favoured explanation?"

"No. It's never my favoured explanation for anything. It is the explanation of last resort, when all others have failed. I have never yet," she added, "needed to fall back upon that last resort."

"And if he was a ghost," the vicar leaned back and blew out a cloud of smoke from his freshly relit pipe, "he was an extraordinarily *solid* sort of ghost."

"The oddest ghost I've ever come across. In my experience, ghosts tend to be nocturnal creatures or at the very least crepuscular. They never appear in the broad light of day. Still less do they make jokes or play silly tricks. They are a very solemn breed, on the whole, more inclined to dire warnings and ominous predictions."

"Yet returning to the possibility that he was ordinary flesh and blood, there were oddities about that too, according to Mary's account. The uniform, for instance. If the army believes him to be dead, why would he still be wearing full uniform? It would only draw attention to his absence without leave. Yet it wasn't quite full uniform, was it?"

"No. I thought about that. Mary made special mention of his hair. Where was his cap? And why wasn't he wearing a greatcoat? It was a cold day, and more so up on the hills."

"Yes. We think alike, do we not? Have you ever seen a soldier in uniform without a cap? It would be like a parson without his clerical collar. I suppose he could have left it behind somewhere, but... why?"

"And why should he tell Mary he had been waiting for her? He couldn't possibly have known she would be in that particular place, at that time, on that day."

The vicar smiled. "It's all most perplexing for you, isn't it? Do you have any idea what to do next?"

"Yes. I shall start with the War Office. I may be able to get more details about Stephen Drake's death and discover whether there is any possibility of a mistake. Now that peace has returned I may even be able to contact his officer or some of his comrades. It will be a long and tedious business but it may clarify matters and possibly eliminate some of the hypotheses."

"You're very enterprising. If there is any way I can help, please don't hesitate. I am intrigued by the whole business. Your approach to it strikes me as admirably methodical; almost academic, one might say. It is a refreshing change after the sensationalism of the newspaper accounts."

"It was a gift for them," said Emily. "Just the sort of story they wanted after the armistice."

"Yes, I can understand that, regrettable though it may be. 'Young woman sees ghost of dead soldier', an irresistible headline."

"Hero," Emily corrected him. "We don't have soldiers any more, only heroes."

The vicar sighed. "I'd never make a newspaper reporter. I keep lapsing into ordinary English. Still, my offer stands. If there's anything more I can do..."

"Thank you. My address is on the card I gave you. If you do hear anything new, I'd be grateful if you'd let me know."

"I will, Miss Duncan. I will."

Chapter IV

St Oswald's vicarage
Abbot's Sutton
Shropshire
January 13th 1919

My dear Miss Duncan,
I am writing to keep
you informed on the subject of Mary
Calloway and her thus-far unexplained
experience. You invited me to do so, if you
remember, and I am taking you at your
word.
There has been a recent development.
A man who served alongside Stephen Drake
has contacted the Calloways and expressed
a desire to speak to Mary. He has done
everything quite correctly, going through
the parents rather than writing to her
directly. He claims to have been present on
the occasion of Stephen's death and believes
he may be able to offer both information
and comfort. Also, he frankly admits that
Stephen spoke frequently of Mary, and that
he wishes to meet the woman his friend
thought of so highly. My information comes
from Mary herself, who approached me
after Evensong yesterday in a state of great
excitement.
The man's name is William Miller
and, having obtained Mr Calloway's
permission, he is due to arrive tomorrow
morning on the train from Ludlow. If his

credentials are good and he genuinely was a witness to Stephen's death then his testimony will obviously reduce the number of possible explanations for Mary's odd experience.

I hope that your own investigations are bearing fruit, if they are still in progress and have not been superseded by other, more recent phenomena. Also I trust you are keeping well and have not been affected by the influenza epidemic, which I hear is particularly virulent in London. If you feel the need to escape the capital city, you are welcome to visit me here at any time.

Yours Sincerely,
Rev. Anthony Small.

Mr and Mrs Calloway were in the little drawing room with Mary, waiting. Mr Calloway was looking ostentatiously at the clock on the mantelpiece as eleven o'clock drew nigh. When the minute hand reached the hour, he frowned and took out his pocket watch to check its accuracy. When it ticked on to one minute past the doorbell rang and his face cleared.

"Punctual," he said. "I approve of that."

The maid Elsie ushered in a tall, brawny man with carefully glossed hair parted in the centre and a thick but well-trimmed moustache. He was wearing the kind of standardised suit issued to soldiers on demobilisation, of cheap material badly cut and ill-fitting, and he carried a soft hat in his hands. Poor but respectable would have been most people's immediate reaction. He stood just inside the door, looking a little awkward but perhaps not as much so as one would expect. There was a confidence about him, despite the socially unusual circumstances.

"Mr Miller," Calloway greeted him. "I was just saying how punctual you were. Please, come in and sit down."

"If the army teaches you nothing else, sir, it teaches you the importance of punctuality." His voice was deep and warm, the soft accent native to the county. He took up the offer of a chair and leaned back in it, resting his hat on his knees.

Calloway, more pleased than he would have admitted by being called 'sir', took up his usual stance and rocked gently back and forward on his heels. "I hope you don't object to the presence of myself and my wife, even though your business is with our daughter."

"Not at all, sir. It's entirely proper that you should hear what I have to say."

"Good, then let's begin. You served with Mr Drake, I gather."

"That's right. We were more than a year together in the same company. We came to know one another pretty well in that time. War may be a terrible thing – indeed, it *is* a terrible thing – but it brings men together, you can say that for it at least. You're with each other day and night, in battle and at rest. You rely on one another in a way that rarely happens in normal life." He looked directly at Mary, as if addressing himself exclusively to her. "Stephen talked a lot about you, Miss Calloway. He carried your picture with him and I know your likeness and the memory of you was a great comfort to him during difficult times."

"Thank you for that, Mr Miller." Mary sounded perfectly calm. "It's good of you to say so and I'm sure you mean well; but if you'll excuse my being blunt, it's platitudes, isn't it?"

"Really, Mary!" Her father was shocked.

"Oh, do be quiet daddy. What I would like to know, Mr Miller, is were you with Stephen on the day he died?"

"I was. In fact, I was by his side until a few seconds before his death."

"Then that is what I want to know about. I want you to tell me what happened at the end."

Miller stared at her. Mary's mother, silent and ignored in her usual place by the window, wondered about the stare. There was, she thought, something speculative about it. There was a look on Miller's face that reminded her of one that appeared on her husband's at times when he was assessing a potential business opportunity. Perhaps she was imagining it, or perhaps not. Her husband often told her she had too much imagination and that Mary took after her in that respect.

"You want the plain facts?"

"I do, if you please."

"The plain facts of battle aren't very pretty. They're not generally for a lady's ears." He glanced over at Mr Calloway. "Your father may not approve of you hearing what I have to say."

Calloway cleared his throat, looking uncomfortable. "Your sentiments do you credit, Mr Miller, but in this case there are special circumstances. My daughter may benefit from what you can tell her, unpleasant though it may be. You see, there have been... certain doubts raised about Mr Drake's demise. Suggestions have been made that a mistake may have occurred. I think it would be as well for everyone if the matter were to be cleared up once and for all. You have my permission to continue if you are willing to do so."

"Very well. You must tell me immediately, Miss," he said earnestly to Mary, "if at any time you would prefer me to stop."

"If I do, I will. Consider that understood."

Miller nodded. "It was near the end of the war, of course. We can say that now, looking back, but at the time few of the men at the front believed it. It had all gone on too long and there had been too many false dawns. It's fair to say the general attitude was: we'll

38

believe it when we see it and not before. In the meantime, the fighting went on much as usual. We were near Ypres," - he carefully pronounced it more or less correctly, not the English colloquial version of 'Wipers' - "which was quite a coincidence. That was where it all started, and as far as we were concerned that was where it ended. All the big advances and retreats in between didn't seem to have achieved much in the long run. But that's just a poor infantryman's perspective, no doubt it looked different to the generals.

"We were trying to take control of what was left of a village. God knows why anybody wanted it, most of it being in ruins anyway, but both sides did. The Huns had it and we were supposed to take it away from them. They didn't want us to, and they were shelling us to keep us at a distance. Heavy stuff it was, big guns. We tried to move forward, but we had a lot of casualties. Eventually we dug in and stayed where we were for a while, waiting for our own artillery to get their range." He broke off suddenly. "Do you follow all this, Miss? You get to take it all for granted when you're there, but it must be a bit technical for anybody who hasn't been part of it."

"I follow it. Carry on, Mr Miller."

"Well, we were all keeping our heads down and waiting for the order to move. You spend a lot of time waiting, in the army. Drake was next to me and suddenly he said, 'There's somebody wounded out there, I can hear him'. He was right. Somebody was moaning something awful. A terrible sound it was. It may have been someone who'd been hit by a sniper and been left behind when we pulled back and dug in to avoid the shelling, we couldn't tell. 'We can't just leave him there,' says Drake. 'I'm going to bring him in.'

"I asked him, shouldn't we get permission from the officer? He grinned at me. 'Not likely,' he said, 'the officer would say no'. And so he would have. You didn't risk two men to save one. It didn't make military sense, which is different from any other kind of sense. Drake

39

was up and out of there without hesitating. It was just like him, just the sort of thing he would do. I followed him and we ran across open ground towards the sound of the injured man. The shells were still falling, but we hoped for the best and kept on running. Then the shell hit. I heard it coming and threw myself down on the ground. I don't mind saying, I'd have burrowed into it if I'd been able. You can tell when it's a shell that has your name on it. It's the noise they make, it's different somehow when they're heading straight for you. As I said, I just flattened myself and pulled my tin hat down as hard as I could, but Drake carried on. I don't know whether he hadn't heard it or whether he just didn't care but I know he carried on."

"Go on." Mary sounded breathless, tense.

"When a heavy shell explodes, it's like an earthquake. It *is* an earthquake. The ground beneath you moves and shakes. The soil is thrown up and comes down like a hailstorm. And it's louder than anything you can imagine. You can't hear a thing afterwards. Anyway, when it was all over I was still alive. It surprised me a bit, that did. I shook the earth off me and looked up. Where Drake had been there was nothing but a big hole. He was gone. In a good cause, Miss, it was in a good cause, saving a man's life. Even if he didn't manage to do it, he tried his best."

There was a short silence. Calloway shook his head sadly. "Terrible," he said sententiously. "Terrible. But as you say, both you and he made a noble attempt. The fact that you lived and he died..."

"So you didn't actually see him die?" Mary interrupted abruptly.

"Not the moment of it, no. I had my head well down, as I said. But he couldn't have survived that blast."

"Why not? You did. Perhaps he threw himself down a moment later. Perhaps there was some depression in the ground that protected him. It's not entirely impossible, is it?"

Miller looked down at the hat on his knees. After some apparent consideration, he said, "Very few things are entirely impossible, Miss, but some are extremely unlikely."

"If you didn't see him killed, did you see his body afterwards?"

"Really, Mary, that is..." her father sounded outraged at the question but Miller interrupted him.

"Miss, excuse me saying so because I know it's not a pleasant subject for a young lady, but after a shell like that hits a man there isn't any body. There's nothing left you'd recognise as human."

"No. That was silly of me." Mary's voice was unsteady and her face had paled visibly. "There wouldn't be, of course. I wasn't thinking clearly."

"You're *not* thinking clearly," said her father firmly. "If you don't mind, Mr Miller, we should call a halt now. My daughter is understandably upset."

"But I saw him," cried Mary, "I *saw* him! It was Stephen."

"Whatever you may have seen, Miss, I doubt it was Stephen Drake alive and well. If he had survived, which isn't likely, he would have rejoined his unit. What else could he have done? None of us ever saw him again."

"But there are all sorts of things... Concussion, amnesia even..."

"Mary, that's enough! You're becoming hysterical. Mr Miller, thank you for coming but allow me to show you out now."

Miller stood up. He still appeared quite calm and self-assured. It was almost, thought Mrs Calloway from her silent observation point, as if he had expected something of the kind. She wondered whether he had read the newspapers since his demobilisation, or whether he knew anyone who had. Her husband was standing at the door of the room, pressing something upon the visitor. She caught the low voices.

41

"You have been most understanding, Mr Miller. It must have cost you something to travel here. Allow me to defray your expenses."

"That's not why I'm here, sir."

"No, no of course not. But I'm a businessman, Mr Miller, I understand all about expenses. We mustn't leave you out of pocket."

"Well, if you put it like that..."

"I do. Elsie, will you kindly show Mr Miller out."

Calloway closed the door behind their visitor and turned back to his family. "That was all quite distressing, naturally, but I thought Miller seemed quite a decent fellow."

"Did you?" his wife asked. "Actually, I'm not sure I liked him all that much."

"Why on earth not?"

"Oh, I don't know. There was something about him..." she tailed off, leaving the sentence unfinished.

"I don't understand you," he confessed. "And what about you, Mary? Are you satisfied now?"

"No," replied Mary rebelliously.

Calloway sighed at the impossibility of comprehending his womenfolk. "Well," he said, "In my opinion we can consider the whole thing over and done with."

As Elsie opened the front door, Miller turned and spoke to her.

"Elsie, that was your name, wasn't it?"

"Was and still is."

"Could you do something to oblige me, Elsie?" His local accent was noticeably more pronounced when talking to the maid in the hallway than it had been in the drawing room.

"That depends." Elsie was guarded.

Miller grinned. He had an open, attractive grin that transformed his face. "I'd like to leave a message for Miss Mary, a private message if you follow me. Can you tell her that I have more to say but I didn't want to say it when her parents were present. Things that concern her and nobody else. I've taken lodgings in the town for a few days and if she wants to hear what I have to say, she can leave a message for me there. I've written the address down."

He took a piece of paper from his coat pocket and pressed it into Elsie's hand. It felt unexpectedly heavy and when Elsie glanced down at it she saw that the paper was wrapped around a gold coin.

"Can you do that for me, Elsie?"

"I'll pass the message on."

"Confidential, mind you."

"Yes."

"Good girl, Elsie." Miller leaned forward quickly, unexpectedly, and gave her a peck on the cheek. "Perhaps we'll see each again one day."

Once outside the house he put on his hat, paused to take out a cigarette and light it, then started to walk quite jauntily down the street. That little episode, he thought, had gone rather well.

Chapter V

St Oswald's vicarage
Abbot's Sutton
Shropshire
January 24th 1919

My dear Miss Duncan,

I am sorry to hear about your recent illness. However, you seem to have recovered in a shorter time than many who contract the Spanish influenza, some of whom, sadly, never recover at all. We have so far been spared an outbreak in this vicinity. Our comparative isolation, in this case, appears to be a blessing though all the indications are that it is only a matter of time before we are affected. The entire country appears to be stricken by this plague of almost Biblical proportions.

I have more news, or perhaps I should more accurately describe it as gossip, about Mary Calloway. The more socially inquisitive of my flock – amongst whom I number Mrs Claypole, my housekeeper – inform me with much righteous indignation that Mary has more than once been seen with the man Miller, who knew Stephen Drake. I do not believe there has been anything to be censured in their meetings except for the fact that her parents seem to be unaware of them. Mary

44

has gone to some lengths to keep them secret, which naturally only encourages the gossips. Poor Mary, I truly believe, is only seeking news of her fiancé from someone who apparently knew him well during the time he was away from her. It is a perfectly natural desire, though it is regrettable that she has pursued it without her parents' permission. It is, however, not untypical of Mary and one must admit that her father would probably not correctly understand her motives and would resort to an outright ban on her meeting the man. Mr Calloway is a worthy man in his way, but not the most enlightened of patriarchs.

I intend to speak to Mary about the matter when I have the opportunity to do so.

All of this, of course, is far removed from your own scientific interest in Mary's experience. You did not say in your letter whether that interest had progressed in any way. I assume, in the light of your illness, that it has not. However, I would be interested to hear of any discoveries you do make in the affair.

I trust your recovery will continue and that we will soon be able to meet again and resume our discussion of things supernatural (or otherwise).

Yours Sincerely,
Rev. Anthony Small.

At the bottom of Abbot's Sutton High Street, just on the town side of the railway station, there was a small public park. It was no more than a long, narrow strip of grass bisected by a gravel path and decorated with neat, geometric flower beds. In January, the beds were bare and there were few people about. It was, anyway, little frequented. If one lives in the shadow of the hills with natural walks all around, one has little use for a meagre municipal park. Nevertheless, as she walked the path with Bill Miller, Mary had a nervous air.

"You know, we shouldn't really be meeting here. If word reached my father, he'd be furious."

"There's nobody but us here," Miller pointed out. "Anyway, he hasn't actually forbidden you to see me, has he?"

"No, but only because it never occurred to him. He would, if he knew." She giggled suddenly. "He'd go purple and throw one of his Victorian fits."

"Why? Am I such an undesirable companion for you?"

"Of course not, but you've met him, you know what he's like."

"Well, Miss, if you'd rather we didn't see one another again..."

"Don't be so silly. And please don't go on calling me 'Miss' as if you were some kind of servant."

"What should I call you?"

"Mary. What else? That's my name."

"Well, Mary, as I was saying..."

"But I do want to see you. I want you to go on telling me all about Stephen and the times you and he spent together. It's important to me. You've no idea how much I want to know everything about him, every little detail you can remember."

Miller smiled down at her from his greater height, the appealing smile that changed his face. "One or two of the things I can remember may not be suitable for a lady's ears, Mary." He made a point of using her name, now that he had been granted permission.

"I'm sure they can't be all that bad, otherwise you and Stephen wouldn't have been involved in them."

"No, not that bad. Just a little... indiscreet. It was a different world over there. Men did things they wouldn't have dreamed of doing at home."

Mary laughed delightedly. "Tell me about them. I insist."

"One day perhaps, I will. If we get the chance."

"Why shouldn't we? We could meet somewhere else, somewhere a little less public, then you could tell me."

"I didn't mean that. It's not the place, it's just that I may not be in these parts much longer."

"But why not? You can't leave now, not when you've so much more to tell me about Stephen."

"I may have to. I'm in lodgings, you see, and lodgings cost money. It's money I haven't got, Mary. I'm sorry to have to say it, but that's how things stand."

"Oh. I didn't realise." Mary was disconcerted for a moment. "I'll tell you what we'll do. I'll do as my father did, I'll... what was his phrase? I'll defray your expenses. You're only here because of me so it's only fair I should bear the cost."

"I can't let you do that. I won't accept money from you."

"Nonsense," said Mary firmly. "I'm not offering you money, not in that way. It's not for you, it's for your landlady. Just so you can stay here and talk to me about Stephen."

"And where will the money come from?"

"Father," replied Mary promptly. "I'll tell him I need new clothes or something. He'll grumble and accuse me of waste, he always does; but he always stumps up in the end. Despite all his bluster, I can twist him round my little finger."

Miller smiled. "I'm sure you can. You probably could any man if you tried."

"Flatterer! And talking of clothes, I know I shouldn't really say it but... do you have to wear that awful suit all the time?"

47

"It's the only one I've got. Provided by courtesy of his majesty's armed forces."

"You could get another."

"Money," said Miller simply.

"Expenses," Mary countered with an air of triumph.

"No, not that. I draw the line there. I won't allow you to buy clothes for me."

"No?"

"No."

His tone was firm, but Mary smiled to herself. He was right, she could persuade most men into almost anything and she knew it. It just required time and patience. Some men, it was true, were more easily persuaded than others.

"We'll see," she said. "Now, about these indiscreet things you and Stephen did in France..."

Chapter VI

Walking up the hill from Abbot's Sutton railway station, Emily was made painfully aware of the toll her bout of influenza had inflicted upon her. The hill had become inexplicably steeper during her absence. She found herself short of breath and her legs ached. A light rain was falling, and the trivial act of holding up an umbrella called for a disproportionate effort. She was not, she acknowledged ruefully, as young as she used to be, Before many months had passed, she would be forty years of age and at that moment she missed the resilience of youth. It took her longer to recover from things these days. It was a fact of life of course, and one had to put up with it, but that did not prevent it from being galling. She toiled up the slope which was largely deserted because of the weather until she reached the crossroads where St Oswald's church stood. There, she paused to regain her breath.

The road continued beyond the church, winding up into the hills. The vicarage, which was her destination, stood only a few yards past the end of the churchyard on the far side of a narrow lane that followed the boundary wall of the church land before joining the main road. After the vicarage, the road she had followed up the High Street with its shops and businesses dwindled into a country track and the small town effectively ended with only a couple of cottages visible further up the hill. Standing in the rain under what felt like an unnaturally heavy umbrella, Emily thought it all looked much more dismal than she remembered it from her previous visit, grey and shrunken, dwarfed by the hills that rose behind it. It was an impression, she told herself, fostered by the weather and her own state of health rather than by any change in the place itself. Even so, it depressed the spirits.

As she stood there, someone appeared on the lane around the church. At first it was an anonymous figure, just an umbrella much like her own bobbing along above the churchyard wall. However, as the newcomer turned into the road and walked towards her, the umbrella was tilted to adjust to the direction of the rain and Emily saw a face she recognised. It was Mary Calloway.

"Good morning, Mary. I didn't expect to see you. Do you remember me?"

Mary looked startled, but quickly recovered herself and smiled amiably enough. "Why yes, it's Miss Duncan, isn't it? The lady with the coat from Burlington Arcade."

Emily laughed. "Remembered for my coat!"

"Not at all, that's just me being frivolous. Pay no attention. How are you?"

"I've been unwell," Emily confessed. "That's why I haven't been back."

Mary studied her frankly. "Yes, you do look tired. You should be resting, not travelling."

"I'm afraid I'm not very good at resting. I get bored."

"Me too. It's always easy to give people advice you wouldn't take yourself, isn't it? What brings you back here? The same subject?"

"The same, yes. I don't like to leave things unexplained."

"You may have to, in this case. I can't explain it myself and nobody else has."

"So things are exactly as they were?"

Mary shrugged, and the movement made water run from the top of her umbrella and spatter on the road surface. "More or less. I did meet someone who served with Stephen and seemed convinced he was dead, but even he couldn't swear to it."

"But you haven't seen or spoken to Stephen since that first time?"

"No. And that's peculiar in itself, don't you think? If he was still alive, I'm sure he would have found a way to approach me again." She spoke with an innocent conviction of her own charms and Stephen's susceptibility to them. She was probably right, thought Emily. "So perhaps he is dead after all. That's what everyone else thinks, isn't it?"

"So are you beginning to doubt what you saw?"

"Certainly not. I know what happened that day and I'll never forget it. You can't alter what happened just because people don't believe you, that wouldn't be right. It's the truth, and there's an end to it. You can't change the truth to suit other people's opinions."

Emily smiled. "I'm glad you feel like that. It makes my task easier. You'd be surprised how many people suddenly change their minds when they find people doubting them."

Mary shook her head decisively. "No. Not me. But I'm starting to wonder whether the newspapers were right. Perhaps what happened wasn't quite... I won't say quite real, because it *was* real. But perhaps it wasn't altogether natural."

"I see. You think you may have seen a ghost after all?"

"It sounds silly if you put it like that, doesn't it? He wasn't at all like a ghost, not the sort you read about in books. Besides, I don't really believe in ghosts. It's just that I can't explain it any other way. In fact, I can't explain it at all."

"We will," Emily promised her. "Given time and information, we will."

"I hope you're right. However, I mustn't keep you standing here in the rain. You'll catch your death." She giggled. "That was an unfortunate phrase, wasn't it? I must be getting back. Goodbye, Miss Duncan."

"For now," Emily qualified the farewell, "Goodbye for now."

She watched Mary go down towards the crossroads where she would turn off towards her home, then herself turned round and speculatively eyed the path along which Mary had come. Without knowledge of the area, she didn't know where it would lead but at first sight it didn't seem to lead anywhere. What had Mary been doing in such a place in the rain? On impulse, Emily diverted from her course to the vicarage and followed the path. It was foolish of her, considering the weather and her state of health, but she was curious. The path followed the churchyard wall for a while, then branched off not towards the town but in the opposite direction, where it crossed a small patch of open ground then led into an area of woodland. The trees were mostly bare at this time of year, but even so their branches offered some protection from the rain and there were occasional evergreens with dry patches beneath them. It was not quite enough to persuade one to abandon one's umbrella, but it was an improvement. The area was obviously used by local people in more clement weather for walks, and it was laid out with paths for their convenience. One path, the one she was on, was clearly the main one with other, narrower tracks leading off it. Emily followed the main path, intrigued as to why Mary had been here but, in the light of her correspondence from the Reverend Small, having her suspicions.

There was no one else in evidence, which was only to be expected in this weather, until she came upon a bench set under a rudimentary wooden shelter of roughly cut planks. A man was sitting on the bench, leaning back at his ease and smoking a cigarette. He was a big man with a bushy moustache, wearing a suit that appeared to be new; ready-made rather than tailored, but of quite good material and cut. His hat lay on the bench next to him, revealing dark, shiny hair neatly parted in the middle of his head. He was quite a presentable man, all told, and he was looking very pleased with himself. At first he didn't see her, but when Emily moved under the shelter to join him, he turned and stood up politely to welcome her.

"Do you mind?"

"Not at all." He smiled at her. He had quite an open, appealing sort of smile that changed the shape of his face. "Please come in out of the rain. It's not much of a shelter but in this weather it's better than nothing."

"As you say." Emily sat on the bench, shook out her umbrella and leaned it on the bench beside her. "Are you Mr Miller?"

If he was disconcerted, he didn't show it. "I am. William Miller, at your service, but I'm afraid you have the advantage over me..."

"My name is Duncan. I'm an acquaintance of Mary Calloway."

"Are you indeed? I'm pleased to meet any friend of Mary's."

Emily had deliberately not said 'friend' but she acknowledged the response graciously. "I imagine," she said, "that Mary hasn't introduced you to many of her friends."

"No, that's unfortunately true. She's a bit worried about her father's reaction, to be honest. I've only met the man once but he did seem to be rather an old-fashioned type. She thinks he may disapprove of me as a companion for his daughter. Not," he added, "that there is any more to it than that."

Miller was watching her carefully now; studying her, even. Emily wondered what he was thinking behind those watchful eyes. His expression was difficult to read and, she thought, was made deliberately so. He was assessing her according to some criteria of his own and she did not know what those criteria were. Suddenly he smiled his transforming smile and equally suddenly, Emily realised what had been going through his mind. She had no evidence for it, but she knew. He had been looking at her as a woman and she had not met his criteria. Probably she was too old for him, and not

53

attractive enough. Certainly, when compared to Mary Calloway, both were true. But he had also been looking at her clothes and her manner and he had correctly judged that there was money behind both. His sudden smile reflected a decision that the money mattered more than sexual attraction. It was humiliating and annoying, but at the same time illuminating.

"Mary tells me you were present when Stephen Drake was killed in action."

"Did she tell you that?"

"Yes."

"Well, it's true. I was there. That's why I came here to see her. Drake and I had been together for a long time and he'd talked a lot about her. I wanted to see her and I thought I might be able to help. To comfort her, like."

"That was very good of you. I suppose at the time you knew nothing about the newspaper stories, the ones that said she'd seen him after the armistice."

"No, I didn't. It came as a bit of a shock, that. I wasn't sure what to say. As far as I was concerned, he was dead. Blown apart by a shell."

"But you didn't actually see that happen?"

"Not exactly, no, but near enough. I don't see how he could have escaped it, even now I don't."

"So how do you explain what Mary saw?"

"I don't. Maybe she imagined it. She's an imaginative girl, Mary."

"She is," agreed Emily. "You may be interested to know that I have traced someone else who was a witness to the incident. Your officer, Captain Kerry."

"Really?" Was it her imagination, or had he suddenly become wary? Perhaps he had reason to be apprehensive about what Captain Kerry may say.

"Yes. He's back in England now and I've an appointment to see him tomorrow."

Miller dropped his cigarette and squashed it into the ground with his foot. Emily had the impression he was making a little time to allow himself to think. "I'd no

54

idea he was back. He was injured, you know. Right at the end of the fighting, it was. He must have been angry about that. If it had happened earlier it would have been his ticket home, but it had to happen just when he'd be going home anyway." Miller shook his head sadly at the mysterious ways of fate.

"Yes, I know. He's recuperating now. I thought it would be interesting to see how his account of Stephen's death compared with yours."

"Interesting? Yes, it could be." He grinned at her. "Officers always see things differently. Every old soldier will tell you that."

Emily took her notebook and pencil from her bag, "I wonder, would you object to telling me exactly what happened? I'd like to have a record, for when I see Captain Kerry."

"Object?" He eyed the notebook warily. "No, why should I object? I've already told Mary and her parents, it makes no difference if I tell somebody else. You could ask Mary herself if you want the whole story."

"I prefer to hear these things at first hand, if you don't mind." Emily held her pencil poised over the notebook and waited.

"We were near Ypres," Miller began, pronouncing the place name carefully, "which was quite a coincidence. That was where it all started, and as far as we were concerned that was where it ended..."

By the time Emily got back to the church, the rain had temporarily stopped though grey clouds still threatened more to come. She paused at the end of the lane, unsure whether to turn towards church or vicarage, when she saw the vicar himself approaching across the churchyard, threading his way around old, ivy-clad and lichened gravestones. As before, he was wearing his cassock with the old overcoat on top of it. He raised his arms in greeting when he caught sight of her and looked more than ever like an angular, animated scarecrow. He was carrying an umbrella that didn't close properly and scattered old raindrops onto the grass.

"Miss Duncan, how delightful to see you again. I hope you are fully recovered... But no, I see you are not. You look exhausted. Most unwise of you to be out in this weather. Come with me to the vicarage and I'll arrange for a pot of tea, although now I consider the matter, perhaps a restorative glass of sherry might be more appropriate."

"I don't usually..."

"A little wine, as St Paul says, for thy stomach's sake. Come now..."

He led her to his home and ushered her into the study where he poured out two glasses from a decanter on the desk. It was comforting somehow to be in that warm, book-lined room and Emily thankfully discarded her hat and coat and subsided into one of the winged armchairs.

"You have no idea how welcome this is, Mr Small."

"I may have some idea." He smiled at her over his glass. "I often feel the same myself after a service that seemed interminable."

"Is that where you've been?"

"At this time of day? No. I can tell you're not a regular churchgoer, Miss Duncan. In fact it was something much worse than even the most tedious of evensongs – and that is saying a good deal. I've been attending a meeting of local worthies about the establishment of an appropriate war memorial for the town. You can't imagine how excited people can become over whether it should be a brass plaque or a stone monument, and where it should be; in the church, or the town hall, or somewhere neutral in the centre of town. As if any of it mattered. It is the memory that matters, not the material form or the location. I dare say it will be years before anything is decided."

Emily sipped her sherry. It was not a good one, but was welcome nonetheless. "And Stephen Drake? Will his name be on the list of the fallen?"

"Ah, well that's not settled yet, is it? As things stand, Stephen has been officially killed in action so I suppose it will be. Unless, of course, things change before the protracted discussions have reached a conclusion, if they ever do. May I ask, do you have any indication that things *will* change?"

"No. None at all. Though I do have an appointment tomorrow with Stephen's commanding officer, the captain who sent the letter to Mary. Obviously, to have written such a letter he must have been convinced of Stephen's death. I shall try to discover what made him so convinced and whether he could have been mistaken. He's in a military hospital at the moment, to the north but not very far from here. I've taken a room in a hotel in Ludlow, for the sake of convenience, so I thought I'd stop off and see you on my way."

"In transit, as it were? I'm glad you did."

"I've also just now, by pure chance, met Mr Miller. Mary Calloway had been with him." She gave a brief account of the meeting, to which the vicar listened in silence.

"I see," he said when she had finished. "I still haven't met the man myself, but I'm told he can be quite charming when he chooses to make himself so. As I wrote in my letter to you, everyone is aware that Mary has been seeing him – everyone except her parents, that is. No one likes to say anything to them for fear of causing trouble, though I fancy her mother may have guessed that something is going on. Her father, of course, is oblivious to the whole thing. His only concern at the moment is that Mary appears to be getting through her allowance more quickly than usual and is constantly asking him for more. I suspect she may be providing

Miller with money. Certainly he has been spending quite freely in the local shops."

"He was wearing a quite presentable new suit when I saw him."

"Was he? Oh dear. When he finds out, as he inevitably will one day, Mr Calloway is not going to be at all pleased to discover where his money has been going. And one must have doubts about the character of a man who would accept money from a girl in such a way."

"Not only his character," Emily pointed out, "but also his motives for contacting her in the first place."

"Yes, that too." Absently, the vicar took a pipe from the rack on his desk and put it into his mouth without bothering to fill it. Then he immediately took it out again to make talking easier. "And all of that serves to make one dubious about his account of Stephen Drake's death, don't you think? If the man is untrustworthy in one respect, then why not in others? I don't like it."

"Neither do I. These things always end up causing unhappiness and trouble."

"These things meaning...?"

"The intrusion of the supernatural into people's lives, or at least what they see as supernatural. Ghosts, spirits, what have you. It never ends well."

The vicar smiled. "Is that the voice of scientific detachment?"

"No, it isn't." Reluctantly, Emily smiled back at him. "It's personal experience and no, I'm still not going to tell you about it. You're as inquisitive as your own town gossips."

"A scandalous accusation. I haven't expressed any curiosity at all."

"No, you haven't. That's true, and I'm glad of it. Perhaps you should just put my present attitude down to the way I'm feeling. When one is weak and tired, one tends to see the worst in everything."

"Besides, no one has yet established that anything unnatural is involved." The vicar put his pipe back in his mouth and sucked on it then removed it and stared at it with a puzzled expression. "Dear me, it's empty. I must be becoming absent-minded." He proceeded to fill the pipe from his tobacco jar, talking as he did so. "Don't forget that you don't yet have to fall back on your explanation of last resort. Miller, however much one may mistrust his motives, is unable to confirm that Stephen is dead and you don't yet know what your captain will have to say. We mustn't jump to conclusions. That would be most unscientific."

"You're right. Influenza has had a bad effect on my mental capacity."

"It does on everyone's. The ills of the body always affect the mind." He lit his newly filled pipe and the incense-like smell began to pervade the room. He may as well have been swinging a censer, thought Emily, and she wondered whether he was in fact high church. She suspected he was, for no better reason than that it would conform well with the book-lined study and the academic manner.

"Tell me," she said out loud, "you've asked about my opinions but you haven't yet expressed one of your own: do you believe such things as ghosts exist?"

"How admirably direct and how impossible to answer. Professionally I have to say that the church generally doesn't approve of the idea of ghosts. Doctrinally, it is most frowned-upon. When people die, they don't hang about on earth appearing to all and sundry and frightening the life out of innocent people. Their bodies rot and their souls return to God, where they belong. However, having dutifully satisfied my professional conscience," he leaned his head back and expelled a perfect smoke ring towards the ceiling, "I must admit that I am not always perfectly orthodox when it comes to church doctrine. Like yourself, I consider it a matter of evidence. If someone presented me with indisputable evidence of a ghostly apparition then I'm sure I would manage somehow to reconcile it with the church's teaching." He waved an arm, taking in the array of books that surrounded them. "With sufficient academic and theological resources at one's disposal, one can find a way of reconciling almost anything with church doctrine."

Emily laughed. "You're a sophist, Mr Small."

"No," he replied seriously, "a realist. You may find that odd in a clergyman, but it isn't. In a monk it may be, but not in a parish priest. We have to live in the world and I may say we see more of it than most people. Without a degree of realism, we would not be able to perform our duties properly. So we must both search for evidence, Miss Duncan, and if we find any then that is the time to decide what we do or do not believe. In the meantime, can I tempt you into another sherry?"

Chapter VII

At the same time that Emily was following the path to find Miller, Mary was on her way home. She turned at the crossroads and walked the familiar pavement without much thought. Her mind was still on Miller's stories about himself and Stephen in France which seemed to have been, judging by his accounts, a far more agreeable place in wartime than she would have imagined. He talked as if it were full of bars and cafés where amusing things happened. He avoided anything to do with the trenches or bombardments and concentrated instead on their rest periods in various French towns. She supposed he did that because he thought it would please her but she would have preferred an unvarnished truth. At least, she told herself she would. The street ahead of her was deserted with the sole exception of a solitary figure leaning nonchalantly against one of the trees that bordered the road. It was a man in khaki uniform and he was presumably sheltering under the tree from the rain which, though light, was still falling. He looked very relaxed, his back up against the bole of the tree, his legs crossed at the ankles. As Mary approached, he pushed himself upright and waved to her.

It was Stephen. She recognised the fair hair, again without the covering of a cap even in the rain; and as she drew closer, there was the unmistakeable face with its friendly, welcoming grin. Momentarily, Mary felt faint.

"Hello, Mary. I've been waiting for you again. I always seem to be waiting these days, don't I? Never mind, I've plenty of time."

She stopped next to him. "Stephen! Where have you been?"

61

"Oh, here and there you know. Round and about. Nowhere in particular."

"But I've been so worried, I didn't know what to think."

"You mustn't worry about me. There's no cause for you to worry."

"But why haven't you been to see me? Everybody thinks you're dead. They believe I imagined meeting you. I even had a letter from your officer."

"Captain Kerry? That was very nice of him, a decent gesture. He's a good chap, Kerry."

"But why should he tell me you're dead when you're not? I don't understand."

"Ah well," replied Stephen evasively, "it's a confusing business, war. Alive, dead, missing... who knows?"

"But..." Mary struggled with the multitude of questions that came to her mind, frustrated by the sheer number of them and unable to decide which to come out with first. Stephen forestalled her.

"You've been talking to Bill Miller, haven't you?" he asked.

"Mr Miller? Yes, I have." Answering questions is always easier than deciding which ones to ask, and Mary took the easy way out.

"Don't," said Stephen. "Stay away from him, Mary. That's what I've come to say to you."

"But he's a friend of yours isn't he? That's what he said."

"He's lying. He always does lie. He was never any friend of mine."

"But all the stories he tells..."

"Lies. Miller's not a good man, Mary. He's dangerous. Don't see him again."

"I have an appointment for tomorrow..."

"Break it. I'm serious about this, Mary. For my sake, don't keep the appointment. Forget about convention and politeness, just don't go."

"I can't do that! He's been most kind..."

Stephen laughed. "Kind? Miller? No, he's never kind merely... persuasive. I can't tell you what to do, Mary, I can't force you. But if you'll listen to me, you won't see the man again."

"And what about you? Will I see you again?"

"I hope so."

"Stephen, that's not good enough. You've no idea how difficult things have been for me. You can't keep appearing and disappearing like a Jack-in-the-box. You must come with me. I'm on my way home, you can come now and say hello to my parents."

"No, I'm afraid I can't."

"Why on earth not? Is there something about the army, about the fact they think you're dead? If that's what's worrying you I'm sure we can put it right. You haven't done anything terribly wrong, I know that. You wouldn't. It's just some sort of misunderstanding, that's all."

Stephen shook his head regretfully. "I can't, Mary. I can only speak to you. Nobody else."

"But I don't understand," Mary burst out. "I don't understand at all. Am I supposed to just close my eyes again and you'll disappear? Well this time I'm not going to. I don't want any more of your tricks. I'll never close my eyes again!"

Stephen grinned at her. "You'll have trouble sleeping, then."

"Don't try to make a joke of everything. It's not funny."

He became serious again. "I know it's not and I apologise if I've made things awkward for you, but some things can't be helped."

"It *can* be helped if you want to. All you have to do is come with me, right away." She was like a demanding child now, petulant and angry. "I absolutely *insist* you come with me!"

"Temper, Mary. Don't make a scene."

63

"Why not?"

"For one thing, we're being watched. There's someone in one of the upstairs windows of your house."

Involuntarily, Mary's head jerked round. Stephen was right. There was a figure visible but unidentifiable behind the lace curtains of one of the bedrooms, though it moved away even as she looked. Before she had finished turning her head back, she knew beyond any doubt what would have happened.

Stephen was gone.

This time she didn't search round. She was annoyed and refused to give him the satisfaction of seeing her react to his silly trick How he had accomplished it she neither knew nor cared. She strode off, irritated, through the front gate of the Cedars and slammed it uselessly behind her.

"Elsie, I'm sure you have more important things to do than stare out of the window."

The maid started. She had not heard Mrs Calloway enter the room. "Yes, missus. I'm sorry."

"Oh well, never mind." Mrs Calloway was forgiving by nature and she quite liked Elsie who was generally a very capable maid, better than many one had to put up with these days. "What were you looking at, anyway?"

"It's Miss Mary coming home. She's stopped to talk to someone in the street."

"Talk to someone?"

"Yes, missus. It was a soldier."

"What? A soldier? Are you sure? Here, let me look and you return to your duties."

"Yes, missus."

Elsie hurried out of the room and Mrs Calloway took her place at the window. It was true. Mary was standing under a tree conversing with a man in uniform. As her mother watched, Mary turned and looked up at the window. Immediately, not wanting to be caught spying, Mrs Calloway moved away from the window and walked to the stairs. She was halfway down the staircase when she heard the door open and Mary come striding in.

The girl's in one of her tempers, she thought with the certainty of long experience. Sure enough, the door slammed loudly and Mary came stamping up the stairs. The two of them met halfway. They both stopped, for the stairs were not wide enough for two people to pass comfortably.

"Mary, what do you think you have been doing?"

"Nothing." Mary was sulky.

"I saw you out of the window."

"It was you, was it? Then you know what I've been doing, so why do you ask?"

"There's no need to be rude. What you have been doing, Mary, is most unwise. If your father knew, he would be furious. Fortunately, he is out at work."

"Good," said Mary. She edged past her mother and continued up the stairs.

"Really! Your behaviour sometimes... Talking to soldiers in the street, young lady, will get you a reputation and a most unfortunate one."

At first, Mary carried on up the stairs with an air of defiance, then the full import of what her mother had said dawned upon her and she stopped and turned back. "You saw him?"

"I certainly did. So did Elsie. And so, in all probability, did half the neighbours. You really shouldn't put your reputation at risk like that. It reflects upon the whole family."

"But mum, it wasn't just a soldier."

"It was. He was wearing uniform. I saw him so there's no point in denying it."

"I didn't mean that. I meant he wasn't *just* a soldier, not any old soldier. It was Stephen!"

65

Her mother stared at her, then sighed heavily. Her shoulders slumped and she looked down at the staircase. The stair carpet, she thought absently, was faded and worn; she would have to do something about it. "Mary..."

"No, it's true! Do you think I would have stopped to talk to him otherwise?"

"I wouldn't put it past you..."

"No. No, I wouldn't. I'm not that silly really, mum. It actually was Stephen. He was there and... and don't you understand? You saw him. That means it's not just me. I'm not imagining things. He's real. He's alive, just as I always said he was."

"Mary..." her mother tried again but Mary interrupted her.

"Did you see him disappear?"

"Disappear?"

"Yes. While I was looking up at you, he disappeared."

"Certainly not. People don't simply disappear. Besides, I have better things to do than stare out of the window all day. As soon as I saw it was you, I came downstairs."

"Damn!" said Mary vehemently.

"Don't use such language. It doesn't suit you."

"I'm sorry mum, but I was so hoping you'd have seen that. I don't know how he does it, you see."

Her mother looked up at her sadly. "Mary," she said, "please try to believe this. Stephen is dead."

Mary drew herself up and squared her slender young shoulders. "No he isn't. I've seen him, twice. And now we've both seen him. You don't see ghosts, do you? Well neither do I. He's alive."

Chapter VIII

Emily caught an early train from the station at Abbot's Sutton, heading north. It wasn't a long journey and she had been strictly accurate when she said to the Reverend Small that she had stopped off to see him on her way, for the train was direct one.

Captain Kerry was a patient in a military hospital that, like many others, was located in the countryside. Peace and quiet was deemed to be good for the patients' health and to that end the government had taken possession of many large old houses and adapted them to its purpose. Some had been requisitioned, some voluntarily donated by their owners and a few had been empty anyway. Emily had been told that this particular one had started life as someone's country retreat, been sold and transformed into a boarding school which failed financially and was abandoned, then been taken over by the War Office halfway through the conflict and converted yet again into the hospital it was now. There was a motor bus service that profited from the frequent visits of friends and relatives by running from the nearest railway station and stopping directly outside the main gates of the house. Emily found herself one of only three passengers on the bus that day, the other two being a sad and nervous looking couple who sat together holding hands throughout the short journey. They were, perhaps, visiting a son and wondering in what condition they would find him. When the bus dropped them all at the gates, Emily strode on ahead despite her tiredness. She thought the couple would probably prefer to left alone without feeling obliged to converse with a stranger.

From the outside, the building showed little of its chequered history. It still appeared to be the country house it once was. There were signs, though, of its current function. Two ambulances stood on the drive near the front door and nurses were in evidence in the grounds. Despite the chill in the February air some of them were pushing wheelchairs about the lawns. There was also an intrusion, puzzling at first, in the form of a series of posts around the grounds joined together by white tape. Some men wearing the blue uniforms provided to injured soldiers were following the tapes, walking along them with their hands trailing along the tape. Emily watched them for a few moments before the truth dawned upon her. They were blind men, using the tape to orientate themselves around the grounds; blinded by gas or shellfire and now learning to cope with their incurable condition. It was a shocking sight to someone unaccustomed to witnessing the effects of modern war first hand. They were official statistics transformed suddenly into human beings. The fact that they were feeling their uncertain way about such a traditionally peaceful and rural setting made it much worse. If they had been on a battlefield, one would have felt compassion but also, perhaps, a sense of inevitability. The setting was a reminder that such things did not end when the war ended; they continued during the years of peace that would follow. For these men and for countless others, the war would never truly end.

Emily shivered, then tried to convince herself the shiver was merely the result of the cold, collected herself and walked on towards the hospital entrance.

Once inside, the illusion of an unchanged country house was rudely shattered. The old building had been crudely divided up by cheap partition walls into narrow corridors and small rooms, all painted an identical and grim shade of institutional green. She was greeted with hard and efficient formality by a nurse who took her name, went off to consult a visitors' book, then led her along a confusing maze of corridors into a small and oddly proportioned room containing only two straight-backed chairs and a deal table with a glass ashtray symmetrically placed in its centre. It was, Emily thought, more like an official interview room than anything else. She imagined the police or military intelligence services confronted their suspects in rooms not dissimilar to this one. She wondered how the sad couple on the bus would feel if they met their son in a room like this and mentally condemned the authorities for being unimaginative enough to inflict such surroundings on people at such a sensitive time.

The nurse left, Emily sat, and before very long the same nurse returned, ushering in a patient then leaving again as if the entire thing was merely a distraction from some other, far more important duties that occupied her. She made no introductions, presumably assuming they were unnecessary and would waste yet more of her valuable time.

The man who came in was tall and thin, dressed not in the lightweight blue of the wounded but in a standard officer's khaki uniform. He was a conventionally handsome young man with a long face, a square jaw, a small moustache and carefully parted hair, but the most immediately noticeable thing about him was that he walked using a wooden crutch. His left trouser leg was folded up just below the knee and held by a single safety pin.

"Miss Duncan, I believe?" He levered himself over to the other chair and sat down awkwardly. He obviously was not yet quite adapted to his new condition. "I hope you don't mind my sitting without asking a lady's permission but the whole business of getting up and down is such an awful nuisance that I like to get it over with as soon as possible."

"Not at all, captain. I hadn't realised... That is, no one had told me about the nature your injury."

"The leg?" He propped the crutch up against the table and leaned forward, resting on his elbows. "It could have been much worse. My own silly fault, really." He smiled at her. He had a quite charming and disarming smile. Sitting at the table with the lower half of his body hidden from view, it was easy to see how he would have appeared to a woman in the days before the amputation monopolised all of one's first impressions. "But you haven't come here to talk about me. I'm told you knew Private Drake."

"Not exactly. I know Mary Calloway. I never actually met Stephen Drake."

"Ah, Mary. Yes. Drake's sweetheart."

"That's her."

Kerry looked around the ugly room. "This place isn't ideally suited to talking about romantic attachments. Is it?"

"It's appalling," confessed Emily.

"Yes. The hospital isn't all like this, you know. There are some quite civilized parts. The old library is still almost intact and looks out over the lawns. And there's a conservatory. Sometimes one feels almost pampered by the surroundings."

"Then why did they put us in this dreadful room?"

Kerry shrugged. "Privacy, I expect. The better rooms are all quite public, people drifting in and out at will. The nurses tend to use rooms like this if there is anything of a personal nature to be discussed. Their motives are perfectly good, though their judgement at times leaves something to be desired."

"I see."

Kerry took a packet of cigarettes from his pocket. "Do you mind?"

"Of course not."

He offered her the packet. "Do you smoke yourself? More women seem to these days."

"No, I don't."

70

He lit his cigarette and dropped the spent match into the ashtray. "So, how may I help you, Miss Duncan?"

"I'd like to know exactly how Stephen Drake died."

"I wrote a letter to Mary, explaining that."

"Yes, I know. That was most kind of you, but I'd like rather more detail than you felt was appropriate in the letter. I realise you were quite properly trying to spare her feelings but your account was rather vague."

"Was it? Yes, I imagine it must have been. One tends to be deliberately vague in letters of that kind. Anything else would be... unforgivably brutal. People don't want to hear all the frightful details, even though they sometimes believe they do. They change their minds afterwards and hate you for telling them."

"Is that the voice of experience speaking?"

"It is."

"As I said, captain, I'm not a relative and I did not personally know Mr Drake. You won't upset me by telling me the full truth."

"In that case, Miss Duncan, if you'll forgive my saying so I'm curious about why you want to know anything at all. What is your interest in the matter?"

Emily hesitated. Kerry was watching her closely across the table, waiting to hear what she had to say. She wondered whether anyone had shown him the newspaper reports about Mary's experience, or whether anyone had told him about them. It must surely be likely that someone would have known that Stephen was under his command, would have passed the odd story on to him. There was an odd little half-smile on his face as he watched her, one that only turned up one corner of his mouth leaving the other untouched and suddenly Emily thought, I can guess what he's waiting for. He's waiting to see whether I'm open with him, whether I'll tell him the plain truth or make up some story to explain my interest.

71

Only if I tell him the truth will he be willing to do the same for me.

"There has been a complication regarding Stephen Drake's death, one that involves Mary Calloway. There was a most unfortunate newspaper report..."

"Yes, I was shown it when I returned to England." The little smile broadened. "Was there any truth at all in it, or did they just make it up the way they usually do?"

"There was an element of truth, though it was much romanticised and exaggerated."

"That's better than the papers normally manage. The stories I read about the war were laughable."

"Laughable? I would have thought they would have been depressing."

"It depends on your personality, I suppose. They were total fiction in any case. But this one, you say, was at least based on fact."

"Yes. Mary does believe she saw her fiancé after the date of his death but before your letter reached her. She's convinced of it, even now."

Kerry drew on his cigarette then stared down at the smoke drifting from it. The smile had gone. "Poor girl."

"Yes."

He took a deep breath and crushed out what was left of his cigarette. "Well I can assure you, Miss Duncan, that whatever Mary saw – if she saw anything - it wasn't Stephen Drake. Drake is dead."

"There can be no possible doubt of that?"

"None whatsoever. He is as dead as it's possible for anyone to be. Physically, he was utterly demolished." Kerry's voice had taken on a hardness, a professional detachment. "I'm sorry to have to say it, but that's precisely how it was."

"You saw it yourself?"

"Yes. What I wrote to his fiancée was, as far as I can remember, substantially true." He looked up at her and the small half-smile returned for a moment, softening his features. "Though I confess that, like the newspapers,

72

I may have romanticised it a little. When one has to write such letters one tends to make the facts as palatable as possible. Many people are comforted by phrases about valour and self-sacrifice and heaven knows, at times like that they are entitled to whatever comfort one can offer them. I for one wouldn't deny them any comfort it is in my power to give."

"So the account of Stephen sacrificing his life to rescue a wounded comrade...?"

"That was true, in a way. Look here, do you really not mind?" He had taken out another cigarette. Emily shook her head and he lit it. "I find it quite difficult to talk about these things and for some reason a smoke calms the nerves. No, Drake did go out to rescue the wounded but it was actually all fairly routine. We had encountered the enemy and suffered a small number of casualties. It had been a brief skirmish, then they had retreated. When everything had settled down, I detailed a couple of men to go out and search for any wounded amongst the bodies. Drake was one of them."

"Was Private Miller the other?"

Kerry looked shocked. "Miller? Good God, no! How did you know anything about Miller?"

"It doesn't matter, I'll tell you later. I'm sorry for having interrupted. Please go on."

Kerry frowned at her and looked as if he were about to say something but then changed his mind and continued. "As I said, it was all fairly routine. I didn't think there was any particular danger. The enemy had withdrawn. There was always the possibility of a sniper or two being left behind but that was a risk anywhere, at any time. No, I believed they were as safe as anyone could be. They thought so too. Then, out of nowhere, the Boche started lobbing artillery shells at us. I think it was just sour grapes really, no more than that. They'd been forced to retreat and they didn't like it so they decided to shell us in a fit of pique. When the first shell hit, Drake turned back. Sensible chap. The trouble was, the second one landed right on top of him, blew him to pieces."

"You saw it?"

"I did. It happened right in front of my eyes. There was nothing left of him."

"So," Emily quoted, "he died bravely in a humane cause? That was what you said to Mary."

"It was true, wasn't it? What else was I supposed to say in a letter like that? That he happened to be unlucky, in the wrong place at the wrong time? I couldn't say that. Drake was a decent man and he was very fond of her. I owed something to both of them."

"I'm not criticizing you, captain. You did the right thing." She smiled at him. "Not that you're in any need of my approval. I've never been in your position and I trust I never shall be. If ever I am, I hope I'll be as humane as you have been."

Kerry looked embarrassed. "One does one's best. It's part of the job and not the easiest part. Writing those letters was awful. At least there won't be any more of them now."

"Thank you for telling me about it, for being so frank."

"You're welcome. Now will you tell me something in return?"

"If I can."

"Miller. You mentioned Private Miller and I'd like to know how you came to hear of him."

"He approached Mary. It seems Drake had talked about her and Mr Miller thought he may be able to offer her some comfort."

"Did he, indeed? That's most uncharacteristic of him. You called him Mr Miller; does that mean he's got his demobilisation already?"

"Yes, he has."

Kerry smiled wryly. "That at least is characteristic. I wonder how he arranged it? He must have been one of the first to get out. He was always good at managing things like that. Do you happen to know what he said to Mary?"

"Some of it, yes. He told her a story that was much like the one in your letter. Perhaps he had the same motives as you for doing so."

"I shouldn't think so for a moment. I gather he said that he was sent out with Drake on that day?"

"Yes, he did."

"Then he's lying. That doesn't surprise me at all. I would never have sent Miller and Drake anywhere together, it would have been asking for trouble. An officer gets to know the men under his command and I was aware that Drake and Miller didn't get on at all well. That, by the way, is something of an understatement. They detested one another. It was a case of chalk and cheese. They were opposites in almost every way." The captain crushed out his second cigarette and considered before continuing. "Stephen Drake was a good chap, most amiable and easy to like, but he wasn't a particularly good soldier. To be a good soldier you need a streak of belligerence in your character. Drake never really wanted to fight. Oh, he did his duty but his heart wasn't in it. He was too... *nice*, if you see what I mean. He didn't wish any harm on anyone and a good soldier needs to wish harm on the enemy. That, when it comes down to it, is what war is all about. Temporarily at least, when there is someone at the other end of your bayonet, you have to hate them even without knowing anything about them. Drake never hated anyone. It wasn't in his nature."

"But Miller was different?" Emily was intent now, pushing him on.

"Very different indeed. He was actually quite a good soldier providing you could point him at the enemy. If you couldn't, if the enemy was unavailable for some reason, then he tended to direct his aggression towards anyone who happened to be there. It goes against the grain to speak ill of anyone who was in my Company, as

75

good a collection of chaps as you'd find anywhere on the whole, but Miller... If I were you, Miss Duncan, I'd advise your friend Miss Calloway to be extremely wary of Bill Miller. He can be a very dangerous man."

"Dangerous? That's a strong word, captain."

"It's deliberately chosen. Miller has a history of violent behaviour."

"Most soldiers do."

"No, I mean violence against... well, not against the enemy. There was one particular occasion... I don't know that I should talk about it. Tales out of school, as it were."

"I think you should, especially if it may benefit Mary."

"Yes, there is that aspect of it." Kerry took out his cigarettes again, hesitated, stared at the packet, then resolutely put it away. "It happened when we were out of the line, pulled back for a rest period. The incident concerned a local woman. Well, not exactly local to the area but French anyway. There were always women who gathered around the rest camps. One accepted it. They er... in their fashion, they made a living out of the troops. I don't want to be indelicate, but..."

He appeared embarrassed by the subject. Emily encouraged him with a smile. "I understand you, captain. I may be a spinster but I'm not entirely ignorant of these things. Women are not such delicate creatures as men believe them to be. Please go on."

"Yes, well, as I was saying one of these women was assaulted by Miller. Assaulted is actually too mild a term to describe what happened. It was a barbaric attack. We never found out precisely why it happened. There was some talk that she refused to do what Miller wanted and some that she acquiesced but that he didn't have enough money to pay her afterwards. The whole thing was disgusting and whatever the explanation, nothing could have justified what he did to her. Nothing at all."

Kerry changed his mind, took out his cigarettes again and

lit one. "If I'd had my way," he said with abrupt savagery, "the man would have been put up against a wall and shot."

Emily waited in silence while he regained his composure, then said, "But you didn't have your way?"

"No, I didn't. My superior officers disagreed with me. Miller was disciplined, naturally, but in my opinion the punishment was totally inadequate for what he did. That woman was disfigured for life and for one in her profession that means a loss of livelihood besides anything else."

"But your superiors considered that one French prostitute more or less wasn't worth the loss of a fighting soldier."

Kerry had regained his poise. He shrugged and drew on his cigarette. "Those are your words not mine, but I don't think you're far wrong. War, Miss Duncan. War. It distorts everyone's values. But I hope that unsavoury little story explains why I believe Miss Calloway should take great care."

"The circumstances are hardly the same."

"No, but the man is. Miller won't change. He can turn on the charm when it suits him but beneath it he's a dangerous man, a violent man and perhaps especially so towards women. You can tell that to Mary from me. If she's used to men like Stephen Drake, she won't be able to handle someone of Miller's type. She'll make assumptions about the limits of his possible behaviour and those assumptions will be mistaken. There are *no* limits to Miller's possible behaviour."

They sat in silence while Kerry smoked with short, nervous movements of the hand holding the cigarette.

"Thank you," said Emily at last. "You've been most helpful, and I can tell it hasn't been easy for you."

"An officer never likes to say anything bad about the men in his Company but sometimes it's necessary. Anyway, I've nothing bad to say about Drake. You can pass that on too, as well as the warning to stay away from

77

Miller. A decent chap, Drake. Sad loss. You don't need to tell his sweetheart all about the details of his death, do you? Better to leave it at the version in the letter I sent."

"Much better," Emily agreed. "And if I may say so, you're decent chap yourself, Captain Kerry. A good man."

He grinned at her. "Good intentions, anyway, I don't know about the rest. Have I satisfied you on the subject of Drake's death? It's perfectly cut and dried, you know. No possibility of error at all."

"So who or what, in your opinion, did Mary see?"

He thought for a moment. "I should think that like many people she saw what she wanted to see. It's a human trait. I don't believe in ghosts, Miss Duncan, any more than I believe in Father Christmas or in fairies at the bottom of the garden. After the past few years, if the spirits of the dead walked the earth we'd be inundated by them. Every town and village in England would have its own spectral population. And they don't, Miss Duncan, they don't. I don't pretend to be able to explain Mary's experience. I'm neither a psychiatrist nor a priest, I'm merely a soldier." Suddenly he flashed a smile at her. "And before too long, hopefully an ex-soldier. But if you're finished, shall we leave this dreadful room? I could show you through the maze of corridors into the open air."

"Thank you. I was thinking earlier I should have brought a thread with me, but I'm afraid I was an ill-prepared Ariadne."

"And I," said Kerry, manipulating his crutch and using it to lift himself from the chair, "am an even worse prepared Theseus, but I'm sure between us we'll manage."

They walked along the corridors, Emily taking care not to humiliate him inadvertently by moving too quickly. She said nothing about it, but at one stage looked round to find him smiling at her. "You needn't worry, I've learned to limp along quite smartly with this device. You won't lose me unless you start to run."

"I won't run," she promised him solemnly. There was a refreshing lack of self-pity about him, made the more appealing by the fact that he refused to pretend there was nothing wrong with him. The one would have been maudlin, the other wilfully false. He managed to steer a path between the two very successfully. Stephen Drake, she remembered, had trusted this man to communicate with Mary if the worst happened. She understood that trust now and believed it had been well bestowed.

"Forgive me if this is an unwelcome subject," she said, "but you haven't said anything about how you came by your injury. It must have been very near the end of the war."

"It was. In fact it was during the same artillery barrage that killed Drake." The crutch tapped along the polished floorboards of the corridors with an irregular, sharp rhythm. "I caught a piece of shrapnel in my leg. It didn't look like much, just a little cut. I bandaged it up and ignored it. That was silly of me given the insanitary conditions, but I didn't want to be away from my Company for the sake of a trivial scratch. A few days later, infection set in. I made my way to a field hospital but I'd left it a little too late. Gangrene. As a matter of fact, I wrote the letter to Mary from the field hospital just a couple of days before they took the leg off."

Emily didn't know how to respond. The fact that in a hospital bed, facing amputation, he had been concerned about the fiancée of one of his men reduced her to silence.

"It could have been worse," he said placidly, "they only had to take it off below the knee. Here we are, the outside world. Cold, but infinitely preferable in every other way."

They had emerged from a side door onto a long flag-stoned terrace that overlooked a large lawn. Emily

79

could see the white tape on the lawn and the men feeling their way along it. All of them wore the uniform of a lightweight blue suit, not well suited to the winter weather.

"You're still in your khaki," she commented. "Is that a privilege of rank?"

Kerry laughed. "Not exactly. It's more that I'm only a temporary resident here. My wound is well healed and I'm not in need of treatment. I'm just waiting around while they fit me up with a wooden leg. It's taking a bit longer than expected. I imagine there's been quite a demand for them lately. The manufacturers must be having trouble keeping pace." They moved slowly along the terrace. Kerry went on, "I'm told they're very good these days. The legs, that is. Most effective providing you don't try to do anything too ambitious, like playing hopscotch or anything similar. Fortunately, that's not one of the temptations I find it difficult to resist." He gave her a humorous, sidelong glance. "It has a positive side as well, of course. They don't expect you to do any more marching around a parade ground, or anywhere else come to that. Marching is the curse of army life, Miss Duncan. It's even worse than battle."

"I confess I find you hard to understand, captain. Despite what's happened to you and all you have experienced, I can hear no bitterness in your tone. You seem to find it all almost amusing."

"Not quite that. No, definitely not that. But if life in the trenches has one saving grace, it is that it teaches you the virtue of endurance. Of acceptance, even. You can't do anything else, so you learn to accept."

"Some things," said Emily, "seem to me to be unacceptable."

"They are but you accept them anyway. You have no choice. Well, here we are."

They had reached the end of the terrace. A flight of stone steps led towards the main drive. The blue suits continued their endless somnambulistic procession around the lawn and the nurses pushed wheelchairs slowly and mechanically to nowhere in particular.

"Depressing, isn't it?" asked Kerry.

"I'm afraid it is."

"But at least we're all still alive, unlike Stephen Drake. Drake's dead, Miss Duncan. Take that fact away with you and tell Mary about it. She must also learn acceptance, however hard the lesson may be. And don't forget to warn her against Miller."

"I won't forget." She hesitated. "Thank you for your time, captain. I hope your new leg lives up to expectations."

He smiled. "I promise not to attempt hopscotch," he said gravely.

Chapter IX

"Captain Kerry," said Emily, "is an unusual man; an officer and a gentleman, a combination which in my experience is not to be taken for granted. He bears his misfortune well and he cared about the men under his command."

"So it seems," replied the Reverend Small.

They stood talking in the churchyard. The ground was wet with recent rain and there was a pervasive smell of damp earth and vegetation. They had been sheltering in the porch of the church but once the rain stopped had ventured out amongst the gravestones and monuments.

"I felt guilty, having been worrying about my trivial illness while he joked about losing a leg to shrapnel and gangrene."

"Some people joke to mask their anxiety."

"I expect you're right, but it didn't seem like that."

"In that case, perhaps he was so relieved to be still alive that by comparison any misfortune was bearable. Whatever the explanation, I'm sure you have no reason to feel guilty. Our own maladies always seem overwhelming until we meet someone who has worse ones to endure."

Emily looked up at him suspiciously. "That sounds rather like practised professional words of comfort. Are you trying to placate me with conventional clerical platitudes?"

"Oh no, I never do that. It doesn't work." He beamed down at her innocently. He was looking even more bizarre than usual, not dressed today in his cassock but in a pair of very old and creased flannel trousers tucked into wellington boots, with a long waterproof cape over the whole ensemble and a waxed, broad-brimmed hat perched on top of it all. He was effectively protected from the weather, but in an undeniably ridiculous fashion. As usual, he seemed blissfully unaware of the effect produced by his appearance.

"Well, leaving aside my own reactions I at least learned one indisputable fact. Stephen Drake was killed in France just as the official notification said, so Mary couldn't possibly have seen and talked to him the day after the armistice. It doesn't solve the problem but it certainly rules out one possibility."

"Yes," the vicar agreed, "which is quite surprising under the circumstances."

"You're being deliberately enigmatic," Emily accused him. "This is not an occasion for teasing. What circumstances? Is there something I don't yet know?"

"There is. Mary saw Stephen again, the day before yesterday, and spoke with him."

"We now know that is impossible. Whatever she may have seen, it wasn't a living Stephen Drake. It couldn't have been."

"The odd thing about this is," the vicar went on without directly answering her, "that Mary's mother also saw him. So did Elsie, the maid. It was in the street outside their house and they happened to be looking out of the window at the time. They were admittedly too far away to recognise him but they both saw Mary in the street talking to a soldier. Her mother was apparently quite indignant about the potential for social disgrace. And I'm sure I don't have to point out that Mary could hardly have stood chatting to a complete stranger without noticing that he wasn't actually her fiancé."

"How do you know about this?"

"Mary told me herself. I happened to see her this morning, walking past the churchyard just on the other side of that wall. She didn't say where she was going, but I'm afraid I can guess."

"So can I. I hope Captain Kerry's warning will not reach her too late."

"Oh, it won't. I can reassure you on that score, though the warning did come from a different source. It came from Stephen. Or," he added as a judicious afterthought, "from whomever or whatever she was talking to under the impression it was Stephen. Is that phrasing detached and scientific enough for you?"

"You sound as though you're approaching the explanation of last resort. Are you starting to believe it genuinely was a ghost?"

"I wouldn't go as far as that, but we are running rather short of credible explanations, aren't we? We know it wasn't Stephen Drake because he's dead. We know Mary wasn't inventing it all – not that I ever accepted that in the first place – but we're sure of it now because there were two other witnesses to her last encounter, both of them sensible women. That also seems to rule out any kind of hysteria or involuntary hallucination. What else is there?"

"I don't know,"Emily admitted reluctantly. "I'll give it some thought."

"Do. Let me know your conclusions because I confess I'm becoming increasingly puzzled by the whole thing."

"At least if it is a ghost," Emily said, "it's starting to behave in a more conventional manner. Appearing with dire warnings and premonitions is expected of ghosts, isn't it?"

"Yes, but not often to several people at the same time. In the meantime, I believe it's starting to rain again and it would be a shame to see your elegant coat ruined. Shall we seek shelter in the vicarage?"

Calloway walked into the Abbot's Sutton police station early that evening, after the short winter's day had given way to darkness. It wasn't a place he normally frequented, and he strode into it purposefully to demonstrate publicly to anyone who happened to be observing him (there was always someone, no matter what the time of day) that he was going there voluntarily and on legitimate business and that he wasn't in the least embarrassed by being there. The latter was untrue but it was important that the impression was maintained. Once inside, however, he hesitated. The surroundings were unfamiliar to him. He was out of his natural element.

The town was large enough to warrant a proper police station, not merely a police house, but the station was a modest one. Once through the door, Calloway stood in a small, square reception area. The walls were whitewashed and the only decoration was official notices, the only furniture a hard bench against the outer wall beside the door. Facing him was a wooden counter and behind it sat a uniformed constable on a high stool, going through a sheaf of papers that lay on the counter. Calloway recognised the man: Evans, his name was.

Evans looked up. "Mr Calloway. We don't often see you here, sir. What can I do for you?"

"I need to speak to someone senior. Is your Inspector here?"

"The Inspector? No, sir. In fact there's nobody here but me. Still, if you'll tell me what the matter is I'm sure I'll be able to do something to help." He put the papers to one side, to demonstrate that he was giving Calloway his full attention.

"The matter? What makes you think there's anything the matter?"

Evans smiled. He was a big man with a big, slow, reassuring smile. "There's usually something the matter when people come here. We don't get many social callers. Besides, you've got a worried look about you."

"Well... I'd prefer to talk to the Inspector."

"You can if you like but you'll have to wait a while or come back later. He usually drops in before dinner."

"No, I can't wait that long." Calloway came to an abrupt decision. "It's about my daughter."

"Mary? Is she in some trouble?"

"Certainly not!" The response was automatic, then Calloway was forced to reconsider. "That is to say, I don't know. I hope not. She's missing."

"Missing? How long has it been since you saw her?"

"Since this morning. She didn't turn up for lunch and now it's after dark. I'm worried, constable."

"That's natural enough." Evans was experienced enough to avoid giving any impression that he thought Calloway may be making a fuss about nothing. "Any father would be worried. I'm a father myself, you know, and I always insist my daughter's home before dark."

"Quite so. So do I."

Evans nodded slowly. "But I'd be a liar," he said, "if I were to tell you she always does as she's told. She's not a bad girl any more than Mary is, but young women have minds of their own these days. Sometimes she meets somebody, goes visiting, loses track of time... you know how it is."

"I certainly do, you have no need to tell me. I won't deny Mary can be wayward at times but nevertheless I'm concerned there may have been an accident of some kind. I want to know where she is."

"Of course you do. I'll set enquiries in motion, Mr Calloway, and if we find her we'll send her straight home."

"And you'll be sure to tell the Inspector?"

"That I will. And you'll be sure to call in and tell us if she turns up?"

"Certainly, constable. You've been most helpful and I assure you I'll tell the Inspector so."

"Thank you, sir," said Evans gravely, "that's very good of you."

Once Calloway had gone, Evans sighed heavily and turned round on his stool. "Bert," he shouted, "is that tea ready yet?"

Albert Lomas emerged through the door that led out to the back rooms of the police station. He was a tall and lanky young man, fresh-faced and altogether too boyish for his uniform. "Yes, here it is. I stayed out the back because I could hear you had somebody with you."

Evans took the cup and saucer gratefully. "It was old man Calloway. He's worried because his daughter's missing."

"Missing since when?"

"Since this morning, apparently."

Lomas considered this. "Hardly the end of the world, is it?" he asked eventually. "I mean, she could be anywhere. Besides, what are we supposed to do about it?"

"We're supposed to find her."

"How?"

"God knows. I just talked to him and tried to make him feel better, but I'll bet you anything that in a couple of hours time, if she hasn't turned up, he'll be back here demanding his rights. He's that sort, is Calloway. His rights are always more important than anybody else's."

"You could pass it on to Inspector Grice," suggested Lomas. "Let him sort it out."

"I could if I knew where he was. Even the sergeant would do, but he's off sick. We're on our own, lad." Evans sipped his tea and grimaced. "You've forgotten the sugar again. Tea's no good without sugar."

"Sorry. Shall I get you some?"

"No, don't bother. The thing is, Bert, despite his attitude Calloway's got a point. His daughter might be a bit wilful but she generally more or less toes the line. And she is given to wandering about up on the hills. There could have been an accident."

"There could," admitted Lomas, "but I still don't see what we're expected to do about it. We can't go wandering about the hills in the dark, just the two of us, on the off-chance she's lying in a ditch somewhere with a broken ankle. Even if she is, we'd not stand a chance of finding her, would we?"

"Not much," Evans agreed. He sipped his tea and pulled a disgusted face at it. "Also, she could just be sitting drinking tea – with sugar, mind you – in some friend's house, though I can't help thinking she'd have noticed the time by now. Or somebody else would have noticed and told her. No, we ought to do something."

He paused for thought. Lomas stared at him expectantly, waiting for the voice of experience to make itself heard.

"That chap she's been seeing, the demobbed soldier who's lodging in Jubilee Street. You know about him?"

"Yes. Everybody knows."

"Perhaps we should have a word with him. What I mean is, perhaps *you* should. I've got to stay here and man the desk."

"But surely," Lomas objected, "Mr Calloway would already have thought of that."

"Show some sense, lad. Calloway doesn't know anything about it and wouldn't approve if he did. That's why she hasn't told him. Mary may be on the flighty side but she's not stupid. Go and see him, he might know where she's to be found. If nothing else we'll be able to say we've done something when the Inspector turns up after Calloway's been bending his ear."

"All right." Lomas turned away then hesitated and turned back. "What if he's not there?"

"Well, that would be more than a bit suggestive in itself, wouldn't it?"

Lomas grinned. "You've got a suspicious mind."

"It goes with the job, lad, goes with the job. You'll learn."

Chapter X

Inspector Grice was an ambitious man. The police station in Abbot's Sutton was really hardly large enough to merit the appointment of an Inspector, and he considered his presence there to be nothing more than a temporary stage in the development of his career. True to the stereotype of ambitious men, he had a lean and hungry look; tall and angular, with sharp, restless eyes and a forward-leaning posture that was somehow predatory, as if he were perpetually waiting for something to pounce on. He had joined the police originally not from any burning desire to uphold law and order but simply because it had offered him a clearly defined career path; it was one of the few occupations in which a man without any significant social or educational advantages could work his way up from the bottom by diligence alone, while the rigid hierarchy of rank and uniform served as a visible demonstration to yourself and everyone else of exactly how far you had progressed. It was not unlike the armed forces in that way, but with the added benefit that you didn't generally have to be shot at or blown up as part of the job. Grice was popular with his superiors for his strict orthodoxy of behaviour, and unpopular with his subordinates for the same reason. It was an arrangement that suited him perfectly.

He walked now up into the hills above the town, following the same winding, irregular path that had taken Mary to her unexpected meeting with Stephen Drake. There was a fine, penetrating drizzle in the air but Grice ignored it. He wore a police uniform trench coat but it was unbuttoned at the front and he seemed oblivious to the seeping damp. By his side walked the Reverend

Small, one of the few men in Abbot's Sutton who was both taller and thinner than Grice himself. The vicar carried his umbrella against the rain, though on the hills he had to fight a constant battle to keep it up in the face of strong winds.

"You don't have to be here you know, vicar." Grice's accent was urban, from the towns of the Potteries, though blunted and altered by years of geographical dislocation. It sounded out of place in the wilderness of the hills.

""I do have to be," the vicar corrected him gently. "Not legally, I know, but morally. I feel it is my duty."

"It's up to you, of course. Personally, if my job didn't require it I'd prefer to have nothing to with a business like this."

"But my job does require it."

"If you say so. I'm grateful, anyway, for your offer to accompany me to the parents. Being the bearer of news like this is never a welcome task. You may be able to offer them more comfort than I can."

"That is also something required by my job. It's not easy; impossible, sometimes. But one does one's inadequate best."

"Here we are," said Grice. A police constable was standing on the path ahead of them, helmeted and shrouded in a cape as protection from the elements. There was nobody else immediately visible, so the solitary dark figure blocking their path looked almost threatening in its immobility. Only when they drew closer was the impression dispelled by a boyish face between the brim of the helmet and the collar of the cape.

"Sir." Lomas stood to attention, the sudden movement shaking a shower of rainwater from his cape.

"Easy, Lomas. Where are they?"

"Down there, sir." Lomas pointed to a spot behind him where the ground sloped steeply away from the path. "They're expecting you."

Grice nodded and carried on but the vicar paused for a moment next to the constable. "Are you feeling all right, Bert? You look very pale."

"I'm fine now, thank you vicar. I'll admit I was a bit queasy earlier, but it's passed off. It wasn't a pretty sight and when you knew the young lady... Well, that makes it worse somehow."

"I understand."

"You'll have to get used to it, constable," Grice threw over his shoulder, "if you want to get on in your career."

The vicar waited until Grice had moved further away and turned off the path, then murmured very quietly, "Make sure you never do get used to it, Bert."

"I doubt I ever will, vicar."

"Good for you." The vicar hurried on after the Inspector, struggling manfully with his umbrella as he went.

The ground fell away abruptly, forming a narrow gully through which a small stream flowed. Normally it was little more than a trickle, but swollen now by the rain it rushed and bubbled over the rocks in frantic haste to reach the bottom of the hill. By the side of the stream, hidden from the path above, were two men standing over an object roughly covered by a tarpaulin. One was Constable Evans, large, solid and rendered bigger than ever by the shapeless bulk of his cape. The other, by comparison, appeared almost diminutive under the canopy of his umbrella. This was Doctor Pugh, a local physician, though he came originally from Wales. Despite his many years in Abbot's Sutton, he retained not only the characteristic small frame and dark hair of his country but also his Welsh accent. Standing next to the massively immobile Evans, he looked fidgety, constantly moving, transferring his weight from one foot to the other, changing hands with the umbrella, as if he had trouble keeping still for more than a moment. The impression was one of restless energy which, denied a

91

practical outlet, expended itself in pointless physical movement. He turned as Grice and Small descended the slope.

"Here you are at last. This isn't the best of places to be kept waiting, you know. Cold and wet for one thing, and then there's..." He gestured toward the tarpaulin.

Grice didn't bother to reply. The vicar said mildly, "I would have thought that doctors, like priests, were accustomed to the presence of corpses."

"That they are, but most of the bodies I see have come to that pass by disease or old age. This is different."

The Inspector squatted down awkwardly and lifted a corner of the tarpaulin. All he said was, "Yes it is, isn't it?" He dropped the tarpaulin again, stood up and unconsciously brushed his hands together as if to wipe off some contamination. His face remained expressionless. "I assume she was killed on the path and the body thrown down here to hide it from casual view. It wouldn't have been difficult to roll it down the slope. Can you tell me the cause of death, doctor?"

"Good God, man!" Pugh exploded. "You've just seen her. Do you really need me to tell you that?"

"I can see she's been beaten. What I want to know is whether that was what killed her."

"It was." The doctor paused, then sighed and relented. "All right, I can't tell you that for certain until I've examined her properly. I suppose it's remotely possible that she's full of some poison or other, or that there's something else that would have killed her without the beating, but it's not likely, is it?"

"No," Grice agreed. "No, it's not."

"I'd be amazed," said the doctor with some pugnacity, "if she wasn't beaten to death. Amazed, I'd be."

Grice nodded. The vicar stared down at the shape under the tarpaulin and quietly crossed himself. His lips moved silently in a short prayer.

"Was there anything else?" asked Grice. "What I mean by that is, was there any other form of assault besides the beating?"

"Yes, there was," replied the doctor shortly. "But for God's sake don't tell her parents that. They'll have enough to put up with as it is."

"If it ever comes to a trial, which I hope it will, it may not be possible to hide the fact."

"You can try, can't you? For the time being, at least."

"Yes," said the vicar, looking directly at Grice and answering for him, "we can certainly try. If they ever need to know, it would be more bearable later, after the initial shock has worn off. Don't you agree, inspector?"

"Yes, I agree." It was said with some reluctance. Grice liked to do things by the book. "I may have to call in help for this, perhaps a plain-clothes man from London. We don't get many murders in these parts, do we constable?"

"Only two since I've been here, sir, and that's a long time. One was domestic, husband and wife, and he confessed to it straight off. Came to see us in fact, before we even knew it had happened. The other was just a Saturday night pub brawl that got out of hand with witnesses all around cheering them on. Not much in the way of detection involved in either case. I've never known anything like this."

"I hope you never do again," said the vicar with feeling.

"So do we all," said Grice. "The point is, we may well need some outside assistance from someone who's more used to this sort of thing."

Evans cleared his throat. "If you don't me saying, sir..."

Grice looked at him sharply. "Go on, man. Say it, whatever it is."

"We may need help, or then again we may not."

93

"If you know something, get it off your chest. I don't bite, you know."

Evans offered no opinion on the last statement, but went on stolidly. "Poor Mary here, she was seeing someone, a stranger. It was common knowledge. A man called Miller, an ex-soldier."

"I've never heard of him." But Grice sounded interested. A murder solved without the aid of Scotland Yard's detectives would be a feather in his professional cap.

"No, sir. As I said, a stranger. He hasn't been here long. When Mr Calloway turned up last night, we couldn't do much to help him but I did send young Lomas along to the man's lodgings. Just to see whether he knew anything about Mary's whereabouts, you understand." Evans paused for effect. "As it turned out, Miller wasn't there. I dropped in myself this morning, before we started searching. He still wasn't there. He hadn't been in all night."

"I see. Do we know anything about this man?"

"No, sir. Only that he's been seeing a lot of Mary and had started spending pretty freely about the town. More freely than you'd expect from a demobbed soldier."

"I see," Grice repeated thoughtfully and glanced down at the tarpaulin. "Has anybody checked her bag, her purse?"

"Yes, sir. The purse was empty. Also, her rings are missing. She had a diamond one from her young man that she never took off, and a couple of others. None of them are there now."

"Well done, constable."

"Thank you, sir."

"There's something I might add." The Reverend Small sounded almost apologetic, as if he were guilty of passing on gossip. "I have heard reports of this man Miller. They are reports coming indirectly from his commanding officer and as far as I am aware they are not confidential in any way. In fact, the officer concerned specifically stated that Mary should be warned against Miller. He apparently had something of a bad reputation in the army, a reputation for violence. He had once attacked a woman in France and been disciplined for it. I don't want to prejudice you against him, but..."

"Had he, by God! Thank you for that, vicar. Perhaps we won't have to call in outside help after all if we can find this man and see what he has to say for himself. I'll delay it for a day or two. In the meantime, constable, check the railway station. If he's left the area, someone may remember him boarding a train. If not... well, if not we'll just have to find him."

Automatically, the vicar looked up at the hills around them. 'Just finding' someone in that terrain would not be as simple as the inspector made it sound. As he looked he noticed someone was standing on the crest of the hill above them, silhouetted against the sky.

"Who's that?" he asked.

Evans followed the direction of his gaze. "I don't know, vicar. Somebody satisfying his morbid curiosity, I expect. News travels quickly and people can be very inquisitive."

"Yes, I suppose so." He wiped the moisture from his glasses to attempt a better view and said, "Whoever it is, he looks a though he's in uniform, don't you think?"

"Hard to say at this distance. Perhaps he is. If so, he's not wearing a cap."

"No," agreed the vicar slowly, "No he's not, is he?"

"Ghouls," said Dr Pugh. His contempt was obvious. "That's what they are. No other word for them. What possible benefit they get from it is beyond me."

Grice ignored the exchange. "Something must be done with the body."

"It's arranged, sir." Evans was as solidly capable as ever. "You can't get a vehicle of any sort up that track, but there are a couple of men with a stretcher on their way. They should be here soon."

"It was the best we could do," the doctor added. "It's only right to get her back with as much decency as we can manage, poor girl."

"Yes. Quite," Grice didn't sound very interested. "You won't forget to check the railway station, constable?"

"No sir, I won't forget. While I'm at it, would you like me to ask around all the houses on the roads out of the town? Just in case anybody saw him walking or riding anywhere."

"Yes. Yes, do that as well."

The Reverend Small wondered, if Miller was found, who would get the credit for it. He thought he could guess the answer but could only speculate whether the impassive Evans would feel any resentment. He would have every right to. Turning and looking up, he saw that the figure was still standing on the crest of the hill. It was definitely a soldier; the characteristic shape of the uniform was quite unlike that of any civilian suit. Whoever it was must be standing on more or less the same spot where Mary had seen Stephen Drake on the day after the Armistice. The celebrations seemed a long time ago now. As he turned, the vicar had forgotten to compensate for the direction of the wind, and his umbrella was suddenly caught and turned inside-out. Flustered, he fought clumsily to bring it under control. Once he had done so, he looked up again.

The watching soldier had gone.

Emily knocked on the vicarage door shortly after lunch, thinking that was probably the most likely time to find the incumbent at home. She had spent the previous night in her Ludlow hotel, unwilling in her still-tired condition to undertake the tedious journey to London and back with all the train changes and waiting it entailed.

Her knocks were answered by the plump figure of Mrs Claypole, stony faced as before when she saw who was calling.

"He's not here," she said, without giving Emily a chance to speak.

"Oh dear. I had hoped to talk to him. Do you happen to know where he is?"

"He's at the Calloways." Her tone implied that Emily should have guessed something so obvious.

"Thank you. Perhaps I could catch him there. I intended to speak to Mary Calloway anyway."

"Speak to Mary? Haven't you heard?"

"Heard what? I've only just got off the train and come straight here. I've heard nothing."

"Mary's dead. They found her this morning, poor thing."

"Dead?" When something comes as a shock, we tend to ask pointlessly for it to be repeated, as if we may have misheard or misunderstood, though nothing could have been plainer. It was a stupid habit, thought Emily, but one outside our control. "Dead. I said it would all end badly, though I didn't for one moment imagine it would be quite this bad."

"You weren't the only one to say that."

"What happened to her?"

"It was murder, or so they say. Some brute beat the poor girl to death."

"Beat her..." In a brief, almost hallucinatory flash, Emily heard again Captain Kerry saying with unexpectedly savagery *'nothing could have justified what he did to her... If I'd had my way, the man would have been put up against a wall and shot.'* Out loud, she simply said without thinking "Miller."

"You're not the only one to be saying that either." Mrs Claypole looked her up and down with a new respect and the stone face softened. "You don't look well, Miss Duncan. I think perhaps you'd better come in and sit down for a while."

97

"I don't know..."

"Mr and Mrs Calloway won't be wanting any visitors today, and Mr Small will be back soon. Step inside and wait for him in his study. I'll make you a nice cup of tea." She ushered Emily into the house, overriding any possible objections by her sheer maternal insistence, and within ten minutes Emily was settled in one of the winged armchairs with a cup of tea that was far too strong and so sweet as to be almost undrinkable. This was Mrs Claypole's universal remedy for any form of distress, mental or physical. A more effective remedy was actually the room itself, with its calm, cloistered, academic atmosphere. It represented an orderly, civilized, old-fashioned world; a world in which the savagery of wars and murders was not only unknown but unimaginable. Everything about it from the book-lined walls to the desk with the old briar pipes neatly arranged in their rack, the battered and comfortable chairs, the pervasive incense-like smell of the vicar's sweet tobacco, all of it soothed the spirit. Emily immersed herself in it gratefully, as she would in a hot bath and gradually she started to relax. By the time the vicar arrived back, she was half-asleep.

"I'm sorry if I'm disturbing you."

Emily blinked herself awake. "Nonsense. It's your house. I'm the one who's taking advantage, sitting here dozing." Small looked, for once, neither ridiculous nor wise. He simply looked exhausted. The exhaustion made him appear older, accentuating the lines in his face and emphasizing his natural pallor of complexion. "Blame my lassitude, though for once you look more tired than I feel. It must have been very difficult for you, today."

"Difficult," he admitted. He made automatically for his pipes and tobacco jar. "Condolence is a professional duty as well as an unavoidable human obligation, but it can sometimes be almost an impossibility. I don't believe I've ever had such an unenviable task. What can one say under such circumstances? Nothing is adequate to the situation." He sank gratefully into the other armchair and started to fill his pipe.

"How did the Calloways react to the news?"

"Yes, Mrs Claypole said you knew about it. You appear to have ingratiated yourself with her successfully, by the way. How did you manage that?"

"I really don't know. I wasn't trying, it just happened."

"Ah well, the good things in life often do just happen. Also the worst things." He tamped down his pipe and drew through the stem experimentally. "In answer to your question, they took it much as one would expect. That is to say, very badly. Who could blame them? It was a terrible thing. Mrs Calloway was beside herself. I feared for her health and called the doctor. Her husband... well, he is not a man to display his emotions openly but I think perhaps he was even worse. He hid it behind a façade of bluster and outrage but beneath that he was a shattered man. His daughter, I think, was more dear to him than he would ever allow himself to admit in public. I did what little I could for both of them, but I must admit it really was very little indeed. The scale of their grief was too large for anything I had to offer." He lit his pipe and leaned back into his chair enveloped in a cloud of high Anglican incense.

"Was Mary... Did you see her?"

"Her body, you mean? No, thanks be to God I didn't have to endure that. They had covered her up before I arrived on the scene. I'm told she was beaten to death."

"Miller?" asked Emily.

"The police are looking for him. They make the same assumptions as everyone else, probably quite rightly." Wearily, he took off his glasses and rubbed the bridge of his nose between thumb and forefinger. Without the glasses he appeared strangely vulnerable, almost naked. He put them back on and blinked through them until his vision adapted. "You said to me on a previous occasion that these things never end well. What made you say that?"

"Personal experience."

"Yes, that was what you said at the time. I have a good memory for what people say."

"That must be very inconvenient," said Emily, "when it comes to the confessional."

"I make deliberate exceptions. One has to. Not that many of my Church of England flock take confession seriously as one of the sacraments, but for those who do I owe them the duty of forgetfulness."

"Can one forget deliberately, by an act of will? Is it possible?"

"No, but one can try. You're changing the subject. What kind of personal experience?"

Emily shrugged. "Cases I've investigated. Fraudulent mediums giving people false hope only for them to be bitterly disappointed in the end. Self-delusion leading people to imagine things that help them deny the truth of bereavement. Even, at times, hysteria that verges on madness. Hallucinations. Fabrication. The list is endless. I've never known anyone who sees ghosts, or spirits, or what have you, come to a happy ending."

"Including yourself?"

"That doesn't apply, I've never seen a ghost. If they exist, which I'm inclined to doubt, none of them has ever seen fit to materialise for my benefit."

"What would you do if one did appear?"

Unexpectedly, Emily laughed. "I'd measure it and take its photograph, given the chance. However, ghosts seem to be very averse to that sort of thing so I doubt I ever will have the chance. They're very shy creatures, as a rule. I'm always surprised by how much publicity they get, considering they are so expert at avoiding interviews and photographs."

The vicar sat for a moment, smoking his pipe and regarding her through the blue veil it produced. At length he remarked, "If you'll forgive my saying so, you use flippancy in much the same way as Mr Calloway uses bluster: as a mask behind which to hide."

Emily opened her mouth to object, then abruptly changed her mind. "You're right. I apologise. Flippancy is awfully inappropriate today."

"It wasn't intended as a criticism, merely an observation. Do you know what you mean to do now?"

Emily shrugged. "No. I was going to speak to Mary again and ask about her second encounter but that's hardly possible now. I can't see what I can do now that my only witness is dead."

"Not quite your only witness," the vicar pointed out. "There's her mother, and the maid. They both saw Mary speaking to Stephen."

"They saw her speaking to someone but it never occurred to either of them it might be Stephen. I may talk to them when they have recovered enough to be capable of producing a detached account, but it would only be to have as complete a record as possible. I don't imagine it would shed any more light on what actually happened."

"There may be other witnesses for you to interview."

"Who? I don't know of any."

The vicar tilted his head back and blew a stream of smoke at the ceiling. It must have been something he did often, for the area above the chair was stained a pale brown. "Myself, for example. Unlike you, I may actually have seen a ghost."

Emily stared at him blankly. "You? When?"

"This morning. Constable Evans saw him too, and he's as solid and reliable a witness as you're ever likely to find. He has a combination of honesty and lack of imagination that makes him the perfect observer. We were on the hills..."

"Wait a moment." Emily rummaged hurriedly in her bag and produced her notebook and pencil. "On the hills?"

101

"Yes. We were standing next to poor Mary's body when I noticed a man on the crest of the hill watching us. I commented on it to Evans, though the man was too far away for either of us to identify him."

"It could have been anyone," Emily objected, "just some morbidly curious bystander."

"It could have been," the vicar conceded. "That was what Dr Pugh believed. But whoever it was, the man was in army uniform. I'm quite sure of that, and uniforms are not quite as common a sight as they were only a few months ago. Also, despite the weather and his exposed position on the hill, he had no greatcoat or cap. It was cold and wet enough where we were, it must have been much worse up on the hilltop."

"No cap? That is at least consistent, even if it is inexplicable. What happened then?"

"I, er... I experienced a little trouble with my umbrella. It's rather temperamental in a strong wind, not very well constructed. It is quite old, of course, so one mustn't expect too much. When I looked up again, the man had disappeared."

"He could just have walked away, been hidden by the crest of the hill."

"He could, yes. If so, he moved very quickly."

"Some men do move quickly, especially fit young men with army training."

"True."

They sat in silence for a while. "You realise this proves nothing, don't you?" asked Emily at last.

"I do. I don't offer it as a proof of anything, only as evidence for what it's worth. Bear in mind that the crest of that hill was where Mary first encountered Stephen after his... after his death, if that's not making too great an assumption. This observer must have been standing on pretty well the same spot that Stephen first appeared; and, I might add, disappeared."

"Yes. And you say he definitely wasn't wearing his cap? Or carrying it?"

"Definitely not."

Emily laid the notebook and pencil on her knees. "What do you think of this? What's your honest opinion?"

"My opinion," said the Reverend Small, "is that you shouldn't give up on your investigation just yet. I don't think this is over. There is more to come."

Chapter XI

"Miller didn't leave by train," said Constable Evans firmly.

"You're sure of that?" Inspector Grice was sitting with him in the small back room of the police station. They occupied the only two chairs in the room; hard, high-backed kitchen chairs with a deal table between them. It was, had either of them known it, not dissimilar in its official anonymity to the room in which Emily had interviewed Captain Kerry, but given a little touch of humanity by the rudimentary tea-making and washing-up facilities that took up one wall.

"As sure as anyone can be. I've spoken to the station master and all the staff. There weren't many people using the train that day, fewer than usual. Somebody would have noticed Miller if he'd been there."

Grice digested that information. He didn't look pleased. A train ticket to a specific destination would have been very useful to him. "What about the roads?" he asked.

"That's more doubtful, sir. We've gone along all the roads out of the town, knocking on doors. People have generally been keen to help, some of them a bit too keen if you follow me."

"I'm not sure I do."

"Well, news has got round by now, news *and* gossip. Everybody's disgusted by what happened to Miss Calloway and everybody knows who's suspected of doing it. It's incredible how many people are ready to swear they saw Miller on his way out of town, in pretty well every direction you can take. Or they saw someone who just *might* have been Miller. They mean well, they're trying to be helpful, but it's hard to sort the wheat from the chaff."

"So you've got nowhere?" Grice's voice was sharp, accusatory.

"I wouldn't say that," replied Evans placidly. "I said it was hard, not that it was impossible. When you think about the people and what they told us, the most credible witnesses say they saw Miller heading West, up into the hills. If it was him, he was carrying a bag so he must have got back into his lodgings without the landlady knowing, probably soon after he killed Mary."

"*If* he killed Mary," Grice put in. "There hasn't been a trial yet, remember."

"I'll try to remember that, sir. Anyway it looks as if he picked up some clothes and legged it as soon as he could. He must have guessed he'd be at the top of the list of suspects and he wouldn't have known how long he had before the body was found. It's funny," Evans added, "how people head for the hills when they want to get away. Seems to be almost some sort of instinct."

"Nothing mysterious about it," said Grice brusquely. "There's nobody there so you're less likely to be seen, that's all there is to it. The thing is, if he is up there how do we find him? It's not a very large area but it's awkward country for a search. What's more, he may not be there. He may have walked straight over the hills and got on a train on the other side. It's a long walk, but if he has done that he'll be away by now."

"We can check on that, at least. I'll call the railway stations, any he could have reached."

"You do that, constable. In the meantime, we must start a search of the hills. I'll get some help in from neighbouring districts, as many men as can be spared. Perhaps we could also use some local civilian volunteers."

Evans coughed discreetly. "I don't know about that, sir."

"Why not, man? Miller's potentially dangerous, I'm aware of that, but providing we take proper precautions and don't let people wander about on their own, no harm should come to them."

"I wasn't thinking about the volunteers, sir. I was thinking more about Miller. Feelings are running high in the town and if a bunch of local lads were to find him up on the hills where no one can see them... Well, there may never be a trial at all, if you see what I mean."

"I do see, constable." Grice hesitated. "Very well, forget the volunteers. I'd hate to have to arrest somebody for giving Miller what's coming to him. I'll see how many men I can muster at short notice from round about. Personally I think the man's miles away by now, over the hills and on a train. That's the sensible thing to do. It's what I'd have done if I were him."

After the inspector had left the room, Evans listened until he heard the outer door to the station close, then he said out loud, "Yes, but you're not him, are you?" He raised his voice to a shout. "Bert! Tea, please."

Lomas had been minding the counter while Evans was with the inspector, but he answered the call by coming in and filling the kettle.

"Where do you think Miller is, Bert?"

"Up on the hills, I expect."

"And what makes you think that?"

"Well, several people saw him heading that way. Besides, it's instinct isn't it? If you need to hide, you make for the hills where there are no people about."

"Instinct." Evans nodded agreement. "That's just what I said to the inspector, but he doesn't believe it. He thinks Miller would do the sensible thing and clear off as far as possible."

Lomas thought about this while putting the kettle on to boil. "If you've just beaten a young woman to death," he ventured at last, "you might not be feeling too sensible."

"That's what I thought."

106

"Did you tell the inspector so?"

"No, I didn't. Would you?"

"Not likely. I've got a career to think about."

"Exactly. There's not much of a career left in my case, but why cause trouble if we're going to search the hills anyway?" He frowned. "Can't you hurry that kettle up a bit? And don't forget the sugar."

It was cold and damp on the hills; most of all it was cold. There had been some persistent drizzle that soaked relentlessly into the clothes, but although downpours had constantly threatened from a heavy grey sky, they had never amounted to anything. There was just the drizzle and the bone-chilling February cold. William Miller had found some rudimentary shelter overnight, a little patch under a rock overhang with an odd, contorted tree clinging onto it with tenacious, twisted roots. It had been better than nothing, but not much better. It kept some of the rain off, but made no difference to the cold. He got precious little sleep, spent most of the night awake and cursing whatever instinct had impelled him to climb upwards, out of the town and onto the deserted slopes. It hadn't been something he'd thought about, he'd just done it. It had been as natural as diving into a shell-hole when the machine guns opened up. You didn't need to think, your body acted without consulting you.

In the bleak light of morning, he knew he'd made a mistake. He should have kept going instead of staying in the hills. By now Mary's body would probably have been found and the police would be looking for him. Who else did they have to look for? They were bound to suspect him. Irrationally, he felt some resentment about that. The fact that he was guilty made no difference; why should they suspect *him*? He'd given them no reason to, had behaved like a perfect gentleman right up to the moment

107

the rage overwhelmed him. He was a stranger in their little town, that was all it came down to. They were small-minded people who didn't trust outsiders. Yet he knew the suspicion was inevitable. He had to get away, as far away as he could. He stood up, stretching stiff, aching muscles and picked up his bag. His damp clothes clung to his body, his hands and feet were numb with the cold, but it was daylight now and he needed to start walking. He had to avoid any roads, not that there seemed to be any in this god-forsaken wilderness, but there were plenty of tracks and footpaths over the hills. Provided he headed in the opposite direction from the town he was bound to end up eventually in somewhere with a station. If he could get on a train, they'd never find him. It wouldn't be the first time he'd avoided the police, civilian or military, and he could do it again.

It was hard going. The ground was wet and his shoes became heavy with clinging mud, an unpleasant reminder of Ypres. At least, temporarily, it wasn't raining but the weight of the bag increased as he followed the winding paths, climbing, descending, climbing again, following in the footsteps of generations of wandering sheep. There always seemed to be another hill in front of him, each as steep as the previous one. He had never seen a map of the area and probably wouldn't have made much sense of it if he had, but people in Abbot's Sutton had told him the hills didn't stretch more than about four or five miles, east to west. That may have been so, as the crow flies, but it seemed a damned sight more when you didn't have wings but were trudging along the irregular tracks. Several times Miller wondered whether his sense of direction had deserted him as the paths twisted and turned. You could hardly use the sun to guide you; the sky was uniformly grey and heavy. Perhaps he was going round in circles and would end up walking back into the arms of the waiting police. There weren't any landmarks, one rock or windswept tree looked much like another to

Miller's eyes. He wouldn't know if he'd passed them once, twice or a dozen times.

Eventually he stopped, tired and irritable, and dropped his bag. Feeling in his coat pockets, he found a packet of Woodbines but on opening it he discovered the cigarettes were crushed beyond use. He must have been lying on them last night when he was fidgeting restlessly in hopeless attempts to get comfortable on the inhospitable ground. He swore out loud, crumpled up the useless packet and threw it viciously into the heather beside the path.

"You shouldn't do that, just throw things away. It's untidy." The voice was mild but reproving. It came from behind him, a shock to his already frayed nerves. He turned to face it, in no mood for politeness.

"Mind your own bloody business. If I want your opinion, I'll ask for it."

The man was sitting on a rock that Miller must have walked past only a few seconds ago. How he had managed not to see him, he couldn't imagine. He must have been staring at the ground, preoccupied. Also the man was in uniform and in the grey light from an overcast sky his drab khaki blended with the background, as it was designed to do. That must be the explanation. As Miller watched, ready to pick a fight on any excuse at all, the man stood up and brushed himself down.

"You've never asked for my opinion before, so I don't suppose you'll start now."

"Christ almighty!" Belatedly, Miller recognised him. "Drake! You're alive after all! I don't believe it."

"Seeing is believing, isn't it?"

"Is it? I don't know about that. I *saw* you blown to bits, I would have sworn to it, yet here you are. How the hell did you get out of that? You were standing right where the shell landed, we all saw it, the whole company, even the captain."

"Well if you all saw it, it must be true, mustn't it?" Drake was smiling at him, an enigmatic little smile.

Miller laughed. "All right, don't tell me if you don't want to. It makes no difference to me. Here, you haven't got a fag, have you?"

"Afraid not. I've given up."

"Just my luck. So, you escaped being blown up and you didn't rejoin the company. Well, I can't say I blame you for that. Missing believed dead and back to Blighty on the first train. I wouldn't have thought you had it in you. Didn't work out though, did it? As things turned out, you're still in uniform and I'm a genuine, legal civilian. Not your fault, of course. You weren't to know the war was about to end, were you? None of us really believed that. It seemed too much like wishful thinking."

Drake walked down to the path so that the two men were no more than a few feet apart. He looked, Miller thought, more relaxed and assured than he had ever seen him.

"You should have brought your greatcoat and cap with you. It's bloody cold up here."

"Oddly enough, I don't seem to feel the cold much these days."

"Lucky you. I wish I didn't."

"You got out of uniform pretty fast," Drake commented.

Miller shrugged. "I called in a favour or two, got myself demobbed early. There was no point in hanging around when it was all over, was there?"

Drake looked him up and down. "That's not a demob suit though, is it?"

"No, it isn't. They were cheap rubbish, those things they provided you with. I got myself a new one."

Drake nodded. "Mary paid for it, did she?"

Miller stiffened, sensing trouble coming. "What's that to you? She can do what she likes with her money. I never asked her, she offered of her own free will."

"Yes, she would. She was always very generous."

"You know, I never believed her when she said she'd met you. I read about it in the papers but I thought

110

she must have been seeing things, imagining it all, maybe even making it up. But here you are after all, just like she said." He laughed. "Shows how wrong you can be, doesn't it?"

Stephen Drake didn't reply. He stood motionless on the path, staring.

"I went to see her after I read the story." When two people are together and one of them says nothing, the other feels a need to talk, to fill the silence with something, with anything. "I thought I'd better set her right, tell her what actually happened. It turned out I was wrong but I wasn't to know that, was I? I wasn't trying to push in, take your place or anything like that. I thought you were dead, just like everybody else did. I thought she might want a bit of comfort, that's all. If you wanted to give it to her yourself you should have hung around instead of disappearing like a bloody rabbit down a hole."

"You're a liar," said Drake calmly. "You always have been. You lied to Mary about me, then you scrounged off her, then when she told you it was finished and she was no use to you any more, you killed her."

"Rubbish! It wasn't like that. Anyway, what makes you think I killed her?"

"You did though, didn't you? You raped her, beat her to death and robbed her. Mary's money and rings are in your pockets now, aren't they?"

Miller glared at him. "You ought to be careful what you say. You're in no position to go to the police. Absent without leave at least, more likely desertion. You know what that can mean. Anyway, you've got no proof."

"I don't need any."

Miller shifted his feet and unconsciously clenched his fists in an instinctive reaction to threat. "Besides, it wasn't like you make it sound. I didn't mean to do any of it. She was just being awkward and I lost my temper. She wouldn't be reasonable. I just lose my rag sometimes, you know what I'm like."

111

"Yes, I know what you're like. I've cause to know. Losing your temper might have been why you killed Mary but it wasn't what made you take her rings or her money. No, you're a vicious bastard Miller. You always have been."

"Take care, Drake. You're no match for me and you know it. Watch what you say."

"Why? What will you do?" Drake's tone was gently mocking, contemptuous, deliberately provocative.

"I'll break your bloody neck, that's what I'll do."

Without moving, Drake raised his eyebrows under the untidy fringe of fair hair. "I wouldn't advise you to try that."

Goaded, Miller lunged forward suddenly with his hands outstretched towards Drake's defenceless neck.

Chapter XII

On the day the police search for Miller began, Emily was in Abbot's Sutton. For reasons she couldn't have articulated if anyone had asked her, she had decided to stay in the area. She had her hotel room and at this time of year there had been no problem about extending her stay. There was nothing in particular she could do either to forward her own enquiries or to aid the police in theirs. She was no more than a bystander. Even so, she had a personal interest that would not allow her simply to get on a train and leave the chain of events to continue without her. She had talked with Mary and with Miller, she knew them both, however superficially. She was a small part of the story and she wanted to know how it ended. There was little chance now that she would ever learn any more about the oddly natural and un-ghostlike Stephen Drake but nevertheless he intrigued her. All in all, she simply couldn't drag herself away.

She spent the day wandering about the town. It didn't take long because there was little to it other than the main street but she went in and out of several shops in a leisurely sort of way, examining the goods on offer. In all of them, she noted with some amusement, the assistants treated her with varying degrees of obsequiousness. Her clothes, bearing and accent all marked her out as a customer with money to spend and she was greeted accordingly, with close attention and exaggerated politeness. And she did, in fact, spend a certain amount of money on things she didn't particularly want; a pair of shoes that may be useful on the hills but would serve no purpose in London, a spare notepad and pencil just in case, a small umbrella because she had left hers in the hotel... Pointless things really, but it seemed no more than good manners to reward the earnest courtesy of the shop assistants.

She stopped for a prolonged lunch in a genteel restaurant just off the main street. It was obviously frequented by the more affluent members of Abbot's Sutton society and served unimaginative but acceptable food in an atmosphere of reverent silence where even the clinking of the cutlery was louder than the murmured conversations of her fellow diners. The waitress never raised her voice above a whisper and the whole room was cocooned from the outside world by unnecessarily thick lace curtains, presumably to prevent the common proletariat in the street from observing their betters indulging their physical appetites.

After lunch Emily walked a short distance along a path leading up into the hills; not far, just far enough to leave the houses behind and have an uninterrupted view of the slopes above her. She wasn't dressed or shod appropriately to go any further. There was no rain that day though the sky was still heavy with grey cloud and the well-trodden earth beneath her feet was still damp from the consistent drizzle of previous days. She could see distant figures higher up; dark, anonymous dots moving to and fro in what looked like some kind of organised pattern, disappearing and reappearing unpredictably as the ground rose and fell. It couldn't possibly be casual walkers, not in such numbers and with so purposeful an air, like insects moving around a nest. She supposed she must be witnessing part of the police search for Miller and was surprised and impressed by how many men they seemed to have been able to summon up at such short notice. It was an unsettling reminder that the man they were looking for was dangerous and they thought he may be quite close. The whole thing felt slightly unreal, a sensationalist newspaper story come unexpectedly to life. Perhaps it was fortunate after all that she had considered her dress unsuitable for a longer walk. She turned and made her way back to the town.

Afternoon tea was taken in more amenable surroundings than lunch, an unpretentious little tea-room at the top end of the main street. She had a table next to the window and the view, like so many views in Abbot's Sutton, was dominated by the hills. It was too far away to be able to discern the police searchers, or perhaps they had moved on and were no longer visible from the town. Nevertheless, the knowledge of their presence, albeit unseen, hung over her ominously. It was a metaphorical equivalent of the grey clouds that persisted overhead.

After tea she walked to St Oswald's, more out of habit than from any definite motive, and wandered around the churchyard. Mechanically, she scanned the headstones when she passed them, as one always does in a graveyard, wondering whether she would recognise any family names. She didn't. Some were indecipherable anyway, erased by centuries of weathering and the encroachment of lichen and creeping plants. Others, the more recent ones whose carved names were still crisp and sharp, were unknown to her. All of them rested in peace, their epitaphs told her. All were sorely missed by loving relatives; relatives who for the most part were probably now dead themselves and similarly resting in peace only a few yards away. Emily sighed. There was nothing like a graveyard for encouraging melancholy reflections, especially on an overcast day.

Her meanderings eventually brought her to the church door. It was enclosed within a traditional wooden porch, the walls of which were covered by a patchwork of notices. Idly, she ran her eyes over them. There was a jumble sale this weekend – no, it had been last weekend but the notice had not been removed. The inevitable Women's Institute meeting would take place on Friday. Emily wondered what the Institute was finding to do with itself now the war was over and at least part of its original purpose was obsolete. Bell ringing, choir practice, weddings, funerals, baptisms... all the predictable activities of any parish church in any English town or village were represented. Her attention was caught by one notice in particular, because Mary Calloway's name appeared on it. A special evensong was to be held in Mary's memory, to be conducted by the Reverend Anthony Small. She looked at the date, knowing it must be soon; it turned out to be that very evening. The idea occurred to her, taking her by surprise, that she might like to attend. It had been many years since she had been inside a church for any reason other than architectural or historical interest, certainly not for a service. But the circumstances were unusual and after all... why not? If nothing else, it would give a purpose to an otherwise aimless day.

Having made the decision, she turned up promptly. It was already dark, of course, and had been for some time. The interior of the church was not well lit; there was electric light, dim and inadequate, but most of the illumination was provided by candles distributed liberally about the nave and chancel. There was a considerable congregation by the time she arrived to take her place discreetly at the back, and it was unusually quiet. There was little of the usual scuffling of feet or whispered conversations. She noticed several men in police uniform, sitting in a block in the middle pews. The search had presumably been suspended for the night and the policemen must have come in directly from their duties, without changing clothes. At the front, directly below the pulpit, she identified Mr and Mrs Calloway. Both of them sat erect and perfectly still, properly dressed in black and flanked by two young men, presumably Mary's brothers. Emily wondered briefly which one of them was George and whether Mary had been correct in her suspicion that it was he who had sold her story to the newspapers. He had been the older brother, but from behind it was impossible to guess either of their ages. Did he feel guilt

116

now at the unwitting part he had played in this tragedy? Was he even aware of it? The Calloways spoke to no one and no one spoke to them. The pews immediately adjoining theirs were empty, they occupied an island surrounded by dark, varnished wood. The bereaved, thought Emily, were treated like lepers; everyone avoided them because nobody knew what to say or how to behave. The normal social conventions couldn't cope with violent death.

The service was as high church as Emily had expected. There were a number of acolytes in white cassocks with rope girdles, one of whom swung a censer the smell of which as it wafted down the aisle reminded her irresistibly of the vicar's pipe tobacco. The Reverend Small himself looked slightly incongruous in full vestments despite the fact that it must have been something to which he was well accustomed. The surplice and stole hung on him oddly; they should have imparted dignity and formality but instead they made him look like a caricature, a scarecrow dressed up for some liturgical parody.

Emily surprised herself by remembering the order of service quite well. She managed to stand, sit and kneel in all the right places. She echoed the responses without difficulty and even remembered the words of some of the hymns, which was just as well as she had neglected to pick up a hymnal on her way in. It was a tribute, she thought, to the well-drilled lessons of childhood that stayed with you long after you believed they had been forgotten. But she could not resist the impression that none of it seemed to have anything at all to do with the impulsive, lively young woman whose body had been found on the hills.

At the appropriate point, the vicar mounted the pulpit and gave a short sermon. The shortness of it was probably its greatest virtue, for the Reverend Small turned out to be a poor public preacher. His voice did not carry well through the cavernous nave of St Oswald's. It

117

was sometimes difficult to hear what he was saying and when he could be heard then the content and manner of his sermon were dry and overly academic, inadequate for the emotions of the occasion. He took as his text a passage from the epistle of St Paul to the Corinthians: *'For now we see through a glass, darkly; but then face to face: now I know in part; but then shall I know even as also I am known.'* It was a peculiar choice, and perhaps not the kind of comforting message that grieving relatives and friends would have welcomed. The Calloway family, like everyone else, sat through it without showing any reaction.

When the service was over, Emily left the church and waited outside at a discreet distance. The vicar came out and there was much hand-shaking and subdued conversation as the congregation filed out through the porch and towards the gate. The little group of policemen, Emily noticed, gathered outside the gates to light pipes and cigarettes, observing the formality of not smoking within the church precincts. She saw the matches flare in the darkness of the evening, the faces briefly illuminated before receding once more into shadow. Someone laughed, incongruously, and the men wandered away towards the town. When everyone had departed the vicar walked over to join her.

"Your presence is unexpected, Miss Duncan. I understood, perhaps wrongly, that you didn't often attend church."

"Not wrongly at all. I don't, but I thought I'd make an exception this evening."

He nodded. "Because of Mary, of course. I hope you found it worthwhile."

Emily hesitated. She could simply lie, that would have been easy but she didn't want to do it. "I found it... irrelevant. I apologise, vicar, but that's the truth."

"There's never any need to apologise for the truth. Some people find the formality of ritual reassuring,

118

others find it hollow and irritating. It doesn't really matter."

"Doesn't it?"

"No." He smiled benignly but didn't elaborate.

"As a matter of fact, I found your choice of text for the sermon rather surprising."

"Did you? Dear me. I thought it was quite appropriate. After all, we are seeing things through a glass darkly, aren't we?"

"Yes we are, but that may not have been what Mary's family wanted to hear. Something a little more conventionally consoling may have been welcome."

The vicar stood for a moment, looking down at the ground. "Oh dear. Yes, I see what you mean. That sort of thing always seems false though, somehow; too much like easy platitudes. However, I must admit that sermons aren't really my strong point. The bishop once told me I lack what he called 'the common touch', and I fear he was right. I seem to do perfectly well when I'm listening to people, but once I start talking, especially from a script, it all too often goes wrong. Provide me with a pen and paper and it seems to bring out the academic in me. However, I mustn't keep you out here in the cold, talking. Also, I need to go and change into something a little less liturgical. Let me see... Mrs Claypole will have gone home by now, but if you have time before your train leaves I'm sure I can manage an acceptable cup of tea by my own humble efforts."

"There's plenty of time. The last train isn't until ten thirty."

"Good. To the vicarage, then." He looked up at the sky and added, "You know, I believe the weather is changing. I wouldn't be at all surprised if we have snow before morning."

"The atmosphere of this room is very relaxing." Emily sat back with a hot cup of tea in the now-familiar surroundings of the vicar's study.

"I find it so, but other people sometimes react differently. To some it seems claustrophobic. They've told me so."

"No." Emily shook her head firmly. "It's homely. Well, perhaps not exactly what most people would mean by homely but... natural. There's no show or pretence about it."

"I'm glad you like it." Small sat smoking his inevitable pipe. He appeared genuinely gratified. "I suppose it's a reflection of myself not by design but simply because I've never really thought about it."

"Yes, that's precisely the point. It's a real room, not one intended to impress but one that does no more than serve the purposes of its occupant. It's honest."

He beamed at her through the pipe smoke. "Thank you. I take that as a compliment."

"It was meant as one." Emily sipped her tea. It was, she thought, actually better than that provided by Mrs Claypole, if not as strong. She put the cup down and said, "Through a glass darkly."

"Yes?"

"You said you thought it was appropriate, but I suspect you meant appropriate to yourself and to me rather than to Mary's family."

"Both, I think. Certainly it applied to Mary herself. The poor girl was most confused about what she had experienced. And yes, without question it applies to the two of us."

Emily nodded. "It does. I approach this subject with some hesitation. This is not a confessional and I'm not at all convinced of the value of confession anyway. But may I trespass on your time and patience to tell you a story?"

"A personal story?"

"Yes, most personal."

He smiled at her and drew on his pipe, releasing a satisfied plume of smoke. "I rather hoped you would, eventually."

Chapter XIII

Emily's story

My father died in 1896. I was seventeen years old at the time, younger even than Mary Calloway. It came as a great shock. I remember him as a robust, energetic man, still in his early forties; the prime of life, you could say, though of course he seemed quite old to me at that age. One's parents always do, don't they? He was a big man with a full head of dark hair and a ruddy complexion. I recall his voice in particular; it was loud and deep, very confident and commanding. He died suddenly and utterly unexpectedly of a heart attack. He was at work at the time, so the first my mother heard of it was when the doctor arrived at the door to bring the news. He was an elderly man, a very conscientious family doctor with a proper sense of duty and he felt obliged to break the news himself rather than send anyone else. It was fortunate he did.

My mother fell apart. Heaven knows what may have happened to her had the doctor not been there. She was the old style of wife who lived only for her husband and family. I was the only child. There had been some complication at my birth, something my mother would never have dreamed of explaining to me in any detail, but it meant she could have no more children. My father and I were all she had, and now my father had been taken away without warning. Only I was left to her, and at my age I was hardly capable of shouldering such a responsibility.

It was not, you understand, that my father's death left us in any practical difficulty. He had been a prosperous solicitor and, in the cautious way of his men in his profession, had made generous provision for his family should they survive him. Financially, my mother and I had nothing to worry about. No, the problems were of a different kind altogether.

They started after the funeral. Before that, my mother was prostrated and physically weak, in need of medical attention but that was something she received. These things were, as the doctor pointed out, only to be expected. She attended the funeral, we both did, and a most sombre and respectable occasion it was. Everyone was in full mourning. There was a carriage, and the horses had black plumes. Those heavy black horses with their black plumes remain in my mind even now. They were, I think, the first of their kind I had seen and they may well be the last. The grand, formal funerals of the Victorian age are rare nowadays. My mother, to my relief which I think was secretly shared by the doctor, went through it all with a calm dignity that impressed everyone. None of us knew then that it was an illusion, a façade maintained for the sake of convention. As soon as the funeral was over, the façade was abandoned.

Quite simply, my mother refused to accept the loss of my father. It wasn't that she denied he was dead. She accepted that, but she didn't believe it should make any difference to anything. He must be dead, but still there in some way.

She said to me once, "Your father was a good man, with a strong sense of responsibility. He would never just go off and leave us like that. It would be most unlike him."

"But mother," I told her as gently as I could, "he had no choice. He died."

"I'm aware of that, my dear, of course I am. I'm not such a silly woman as you think me. But even so, he's still with us. He wouldn't ever desert us."

123

She was perfectly calm about it, there were no hysterics or anything of that sort. In fact, she was more calm than I had ever known her. Normally she was a woman who tended to worry and fret over trivia, over things that didn't matter at all, but now she was... almost serene in her total confidence. I had no idea what to do about it. I consulted the doctor without telling her, but he had nothing to offer. It was, I suppose, outside his sphere of competence. The best he could manage was to tell me it would probably pass off with time, and that I should be patient.

I *was* patient, to the best of my ability. But it didn't pass. It got worse.

To begin with, she started to consult spiritualists and mediums in the hope they would be able to put her into contact with my father. She was completely convinced that my father was still around and that all that was needed was some means of communicating with him.

The people she saw were frauds and mountebanks of the worst sort. Their deceit was breathtaking. Many of them hadn't even done their homework properly. They got my father's habits wrong, or his profession; sometimes, even his name. Occasionally they came to our house, but more often she went to visit them in places where they could control their illusions more convincingly, and she always took me with her. Even if she hadn't, I would have insisted on going if only to prevent her from throwing ridiculous amounts of money at them. I sat for many hours in darkened rooms, watching what were often crude and transparent tricks designed to part the bereaved and desperate from their money. At times, the tricks were so blatant that I exposed them on the spot, unable to control my anger and contempt for such despicable behaviour. It upset my mother when I did that, but afterwards she would thank me for saving her from a charlatan and then go on in her serene way to another, more sophisticated charlatan. Her confidence was never dented by experience. She always believed she had just chosen the wrong medium and that the next one would be genuine.

It was a dreadful time. For a young woman of the age I was at the time, it was terrible. The strain was enormous and there seemed to be no end to it. Yet it did end, and what came after it was worse.

One day, mother said to me, "You were quite right, dear. I should have trusted you. These people are of no use at all. I shan't see any more of them." I was delighted, as you can imagine. My relief was enormous. It was also short-lived. She went on placidly, "They are completely unnecessary. I don't need them in order to speak to your father. I can see and talk to him without them."

And that was what happened.

She began to see my father in the house, and to hold conversations with him. She would call me in to 'say hello' as she put it. I didn't know what do do. The trouble was, it made her so happy. She had her husband back and her life was complete once more, just as it used to be. I couldn't bring myself to disillusion her. There was nobody there, of course. How could there be? My father was dead. Yet she was so happy...

I pretended. Perhaps I shouldn't have, I don't know. It may have been wrong of me, but I couldn't think of anything else to do. I took part in imaginary conversations. I smiled at vacant chairs and pretended there was someone in the empty room because to do so pleased my mother. Should I have done something else? Possibly, but I was so young. I couldn't bring myself to do otherwise. You can have no idea what it was like to live with that degree of illusion. I was constantly terrified that she would start chatting to my father in the local shops, or in the street, but she never did. If she had, my fear was that someone would realise what was happening and she would end her life in an asylum. But the delusion was always confined to our home, so no one else ever suspected anything. It never even happened when any of

125

the maids were present. It was only ever mother or the two of us, never anyone else.

It went on for months, until her death.

Her death in the end was completely unrelated. She didn't die of a broken heart, or of any mental disturbance or physical illness. She was, in fact, perfectly healthy in every way except for her delusion. It was a stupid accident. One morning the horse of a delivery cart was startled by the excited barking of a dog and took fright, bolting along the street just as my mother stepped off the kerb. Could there be anything more fortuitous, more absurd?

So I was left alone, orphaned at the age of eighteen. My mother had been no support for me since my father's death; it had been the other way round, in fact. Nevertheless, she had been *there*. She had existed and her physical presence had been enough to afford me some kind of security and continuity. Now there was nothing.

Nature, they say, abhors a vacuum and the mental and emotional vacuum left by my mother's death was filled by doubts and speculations. I began to wonder, as I assumed my new responsibilities for the servants and the running of the household such as it was, whether I had been right in my attitude towards my mother's delusions. First of all, I wondered whether I had been right to humour her, to join in and effectively encourage her belief that my father was still present in some way. Perhaps I should have consulted the doctor, or someone else with more experience of such matters. That was the first step, and it preoccupied me for several weeks, until after the funeral. Then I began to wonder about something more fundamental. I began to question whether or not I had been correct in my assumptions about the nature of my mother's experience.

The thought that took root in my mind was disturbing. It was that I may have been too confident in my interpretation of my mother's behaviour. When there are two people and one of them sees something the other doesn't, there is more than one possible explanation of what is happening. The first, and the one I had assumed to be true, is that one person is hallucinating, is seeing things that are not real. The other, which had never even occurred to me at the time, is that one person actually does see something but for some reason the other person is unable to see it. Had my mother actually seen something, experienced something, that I had been unable to share?

You can perhaps imagine how unsettling such a thought was to me. Yet I couldn't rid myself of it, it stayed with me and gradually grew larger in my mind.

I should say at this point that I was reasonably well educated for a woman of that era. My father had been a firm believer in the value of education for both men and women alike, and I had been provided as a girl with several tutors and a a generous supply of carefully selected books. I did not entirely conform to the conventional image of frivolous femininity. However, neither was I accustomed to the habit of rigorous research and abstract reasoning; my education had been largely limited to the learning of facts. I possessed, I believe, the inclination for it, but not the training. Therefore the ideas that began to preoccupy me were slow in their evolution.

I began looking for books, articles, anything relating to the subject of ghosts, of survival after death, of the whole treacherous and nebulous area of supernatural experience. There was an enormous amount of it. I couldn't believe at first how much had been written, much of it fairly recent. The subject seemed to be a popular one, which went some way towards explaining how my mother had found it so easy to discover one medium after another. Spiritualists seemed to be established in almost every town in the country. People were making a dubious living out of the very doubts that had begun to assail me, and out of the grief that had overwhelmed my mother. A great deal of the literature, like most of the mediums, was vague and unconvincing though I found just enough odd stories and accounts to prevent me from abandoning the subject.

Quite quickly I also discovered that a number of societies existed to cater for people who were pursuing this interest. I joined several of the more serious ones – those that would accept women as members, that is, which was by no means all of them. This in turn enabled me to contact and correspond with other people who had been involved with the subject for longer than I and who knew far more about it. I also gained enough confidence to venture into the field, as it were, to interview people whose experiences had been related to me by others. They turned out to be as varied a collection of people as you could imagine; some hungry for attention, some clearly gullible and deluded, some sly and deceitful, a few sensible and level-headed. The latter were a minority and were always the ones most reluctant to speak about their experiences.

Over time, what had started as an attempt to answer one question, as mere curiosity if you like, grew into almost a full-time occupation. I had no need to earn a living, thanks to my father's foresight, so I was free to spend my time as I wished and the more of it I spent investigating psychical phenomena, the more fascinated I became by the whole subject; the range of people, the theories (both the intriguing ones and those that were just plain silly), the strange stories I heard, the possible explanations...

And that is how you find me occupied now. I still do the same things, all these years on, and I'm afraid I still haven't found a convincing answer to the question that started it all. I once told you that it was all a matter of academic interest, that it was done in a spirit of scientific enquiry. I wasn't lying to you. What I said was true, and has become more true as the years have passed. But I now admit to you that it was not the whole truth.

I would still like to know if it was even remotely possible that my mother genuinely did see my father's ghost. And I still *don't* know.

Chapter XIV

"Well, well." The vicar took his pipe from his mouth and studied it carefully before putting it back. "I thank you, Miss Duncan, for your confidence. I am most reassured by what you have told me."

"Are you?"

"Yes indeed. I knew there must be some personal history behind your choice of occupation. I hope you don't think I pressed you too hard for it but I wanted to be certain it wasn't something that would prejudice your judgement. I see now that it's not."

"You didn't press me at all. You were perfectly tactful. My confession was entirely voluntary."

"As all confessions should be, of course. The thing is, Miss Duncan, the Calloways are my parishioners and I feel a sense of duty towards them. I also liked Mary very much and would not want anything to happen that would unnecessarily besmirch her memory. My impression has always been that your enquiries would be scrupulously fair and exact, with no axe to grind. But impressions are notoriously unreliable and I needed to be sure. Now, I am sure. So, as I said, I thank you."

"It was actually a relief to tell someone," Emily admitted. "I never have, until now. It's surprising how much better it can make you feel."

"Not so surprising. That's what confessions are for." He smiled at her benignly.

"That's all very well, but in the end it doesn't get me any further, does it? Mary is dead and there is no one who can confirm or deny what she said. I'm left with yet another anecdote that will never be proved or disproved. One of many."

"Don't be so certain of that. As I said to you before, the story isn't over yet. But talking of things being over, you should be making your way to the station if you're to catch your train. The weather, as I predicted, is changing." He pointed with the stem of his pipe towards the window. The curtains were open and outside Emily could see flakes of snow drifting lazily towards the ground.

"Good heavens! You were quite right, though I didn't think it would start so soon. Yes, I must be going." She stood, and the vicar immediately stood up with her.

"Allow me to escort you to the station."

"There's no need. I only have to walk down the high street."

"I would feel happier if I did. People are nervous lately. They are staying indoors after dark and the vagaries of the weather will only encourage that tendency. Besides, I have an umbrella."

Emily laughed. "One that turns inside out in the wind. You told me. I have one too, that I bought earlier today in the town. It's probably far more effective."

"In that case, you can protect me rather than vice versa."

"And if there *is* a brutal murderer roaming the streets?"

"Then we can protect one another. If nothing else, two voices shout louder than one to raise the alarm. Also, I find a clerical collar is remarkably effective at deterring potential assailants."

In the end, Emily conceded gracefully and they walked down the main road together under their respective umbrellas. On the platform, the vicar said to her, "Don't forget what I said, will you? It's not over yet. I'll be seeing you again, I hope."

"Yes. I'll be back tomorrow."

"Good."

As the train pulled out, Emily looked out of the window. The vicar was still standing on the platform, tall,

131

angular and scarecrow-like, waving. As she watched, his umbrella was taken by a gust of wind and wrenched itself inside out. Emily settled back in her seat and laughed.

By morning the snow was almost gone from the town, obliterated by the pressure of feet, hooves and wheels. On the hills it remained largely undisturbed, a light covering preserved by the cold. Hills always look startlingly different under snow, no matter how insubstantial the quantity. Outlines are blurred, edges softened, colours muted by a monochrome uniformity of black and white under a grey sky. The police were still busy, despite the snow, and the exception to the undisturbed nature of the covering was around the corpse of William Miller. There, the snow had been trampled into slush by large, official boots.

"How long has he been here?" demanded Inspector Grice. He stood staring down at the body, accompanied by Dr Pugh and three constables.

"Since before the snow at any rate," offered Constable Evans. "There were no footprints anywhere when we first found him, not even his own."

"And now there are just police boots," said Grice grimly.

If Evans thought 'what else were we supposed to do?', he didn't say it out loud.

"My guess," said Pugh, "would be that he's been here about twenty four hours, give or take a little. Since yesterday morning some time."

"Guess? Is that the best you can do, a guess?"

"At the moment, yes. What else do you expect, man? This isn't a laboratory, it's an exposed hillside. And a bloody cold one too, come to that," he added grouchily. He was fidgeting and shifting his weight from foot to foot, though whether that was because of the cold or because of his habitual restlessness wasn't clear.

"So what killed him?"

"How should I know?" snapped the doctor. "There are no signs of assault, no bleeding. I'll need to examine him before I can say any more than that."

"Can't you examine him now?"

"Here? Don't talk like a fool, man."

Grice stooped and studied the body more closely. "What can have caused those burns on his hands? They look as severe as anything I've ever seen."

The hands were ugly, twisted and disfigured by purple and black blisters.

"They're not burns," said Pugh tersely. "A typical layman's diagnosis. They look a bit like burns, so they must *be* burns. Well, they're not."

"So what are they?" demanded Grice irritably. "What's your expert opinion?"

Pugh glared at him. "Frostbite," he said.

"Frostbite? Surely it can't have been cold enough overnight to cause frostbite?"

"Cold enough? Here?" The doctor's tone was contemptuous. "To get frostbite that severe he'd need to have been waving his hands about in the Antarctic for weeks, without benefit of gloves. I doubt if even Captain Scott had frostbite that badly. Cold enough, indeed!"

"Then what caused it?"

"How on earth should I know? I can tell you what it is but I can't tell you how he got it. I'm not psychic, man. It wouldn't have killed him anyway, I can tell you that much. If he'd still been alive I'd probably have been amputating his hands, but he isn't so I won't. There's that to be grateful for, at least."

"I doubt *he* feels very grateful," snapped Grice.

"*He* doesn't feel anything at all," Pugh retorted. "He's dead."

"Thank you for that diagnosis. And what are you going to put on the death certificate as the cause of death?"

"God knows. If I so much as mention frostbite, I'll be laughed out of court." He thought about it for a few moments. "Unless I find anything else," he said at last, "it will probably be heart failure."

"Heart failure?" Grice was incredulous. "Would that be true?"

"Would I lie on a death certificate? I've got my reputation to think of. Naturally it would be true. It's always true. That's what everybody dies of. Their hearts stop beating and they die, it's as simple as that." He pointed down at the contorted body. "His heart's not beating, is it? And he's dead, isn't he? Well, there you are then."

Grice stared at him in disbelief, opened his mouth to reply then realised he could think of nothing to say and closed it again. He turned on his heel and strode off down the hill without a word. When he was out of earshot, Pugh turned to Evans and said, "I can't resist it, you know. The man asks for it. Too high and mighty by half, he is."

Evans kept a straight face. "That's most reprehensible of you, sir."

Pugh grinned wickedly. "Yes, isn't it?"

"Was it really heart failure that killed him?" Evans asked. "Just between the two of us, that is."

"I haven't the faintest idea what killed him," admitted the doctor, "So yes, it most likely was. Unless you can think of anything better."

Evans shook his head. "To be honest, I can't think of anything at all. It just doesn't look at all natural to my way of thinking."

"No. It doesn't, does it?

At the time Miller's body was discovered, Emily was eating breakfast in her hotel. It was a good hotel in a good position, overlooking Ludlow town square, and it was a good breakfast. Her enjoyment of it was cut short by one of the waiters, who approached her table to murmur discreetly, "There's a gentleman asking to see you, Miss. He's waiting in the lounge."

"A gentleman? What sort of gentleman?" The hotel was of the type to be unused to men visiting female guests. The fact that he had been described as a gentleman, and that they had informed her of his presence, must mean that the management had not had any reason to take exception to this particular visitor.

"An officer, Miss." That explained it.

"I see. Well, please tell him I'll join him shortly, when I've finished here."

"Certainly, Miss."

She hurried the remainder of her breakfast – which was a waste, but necessary – and walked to the lounge. It was a small but comfortable room at the front of the building, heavy with genuinely dark old beams, furnished for relaxation and having one large and mullioned window offering a view of the square. The only person in it stood as she entered and threw the cigarette he had been smoking into the fireplace. He had been settled in a low, soft armchair and standing obviously presented him with some difficulties which he tried unsuccessfully to conceal. He achieved it with the aid of a walking stick and the added support of the arms of the chair.

"Please, Captain Kerry. There's no need for formality. I'm surprised to see you here."

"Are you? You don't sound it."

"Well, I was informed it was an officer and I haven't met many officers recently so you were the most likely candidate. However, I can't imagine how you traced me to this place."

135

He subsided back into his chair and grinned at her. "It wasn't difficult. If you remember, you left me one of your very elegant and impressive calling cards. When the people at the hospital told me I could leave, I simply rang the telephone number on the card."

"And they told you where to find me?"

"Eventually. You mustn't be too hard on your staff. I gave them my rank and my address at the military hospital, and they took pity on me. I took shameless advantage, I'm afraid. An officer's uniform and a conspicuous war wound will get you anywhere these days. It's almost the equivalent of what a title and a top hat were before the war. Even the staff here at your most respectable hotel deferred to me when they saw me limping about and looking suitably heroic."

Despite herself, Emily laughed. "Shameless is the right word."

He looked around him. "I say, it's rather better than the environment of our last meeting, isn't it?"

"Anything would be. How is the leg, if you don't mind my asking?"

"Oh, not too bad. It's rather awkward still, and sore at times but they warned me that would happen. I can get about pretty well, though, with the aid of the stick." He patted the top of the walking stick that he had leaned against the chair, then added, "No hopscotch, though."

"Very wise of you."

"Wisdom is sometimes the child of necessity. I say, that was rather good on the spur of the moment, don't you think?"

"I think," said Emily, "that a friend recently told me I used frivolity as a mask. I'm not the only one, am I?"

There was a short silence, then Kerry said quietly, "It's infinitely better than self-pity though, isn't it?"

"It is. I didn't mean it as a criticism. Now, you've told me *how* you found me but you haven't told me *why* you did so. I'm intrigued. Have you thought of something

136

you forgot to tell me? If so, it was extremely noble of you to gone to so much effort to rectify the omission."

"Ah well... Not exactly that. no. The thing is, I couldn't stop myself thinking about what you said when you came to visit me, about Mary Calloway and her odd experience, and most of all about Miller having turned up. That worried me. Call it a premonition if you like, but I feared nothing good would come of it. That man is trouble and always has been. I know I asked you to warn Mary and I was sure you would have done so, but once I was more or less mobile I thought it may be a good idea to visit her myself and deliver the warning in person."

"That was good of you."

He looked embarrassed. "Oh, not really. I just thought the uniform and the wound may work their usual magic and what I said may be taken more seriously, especially as I was Drake's commanding officer. The patrician touch, you know. Also, if he was still in the area I thought I may be able to deliver a rather less tactful warning to Miller himself. Tell him in no uncertain terms to clear off and leave her alone, in fact. However, I don't know the young lady and I wasn't sure how my interference would be received by her or her family so I thought I'd contact you first and reconnoitre the ground, as it were. Ask your opinion."

Emily sat in silence for a moment. He didn't know, of course. There was no reason why he should. "My opinion," she said slowly, "is that it was an excellent and generous idea on your part. However, I'm afraid events have moved on and you're too late."

"Too late?" He frowned. "What do you mean?"

"Mary Calloway is dead. You could still try to deliver your warning to Miller but you would have to find him first, and I'm afraid you'd face some hard competition in that enterprise. The police are looking for him too."

"I see." He sat still, staring past her into space and thinking. Then, abruptly, he burst out, "Damn! Sorry," he added hurriedly, "not decent language I know, but..."

"It was entirely appropriate and could have been far worse without causing offence."

"That man should have been shot in France. Why is it that all the wrong people die?"

"I don't know. Nobody knows."

"No, I suppose not. I should be used to it by now, but occasionally it still jumps out and takes you by surprise. The police suspect Miller, then?"

"They do."

"And how, if it's not too difficult a subject, how did Mary die?"

"She was beaten to death, apparently after being... assaulted in other ways."

"Dear God! The poor girl. I expect she refused to give him whatever it he wanted, either money or something else." Absently, he felt in his pockets and brought out and lit another cigarette without his usual polite request for permission. It was an entirely automatic action. Afterwards he looked down at the cigarette as if slightly surprised to find it smouldering in his hand. He looked up again at Emily and opened his mouth to speak. She forestalled him.

"No, of course I don't mind. Please don't bother to ask in future."

"I won't. Habit, you know." It wasn't entirely clear whether he was referring to his smoking or his asking permission for it of a lady. "So my intentions are rendered useless. In that case, perhaps something I had meant to give her should instead be given to you. You may know someone who would find it of value, perhaps some relative of Stephen Drake." He reached inside his tunic and brought out an envelope that he offered to Emily. She quickly stood and went over to take it from him, so that he wouldn't need to go through the effort of standing himself. On opening it, she found a half-plate

138

photographic print. "It's a picture of Drake's platoon section," Kerry explained. "It was taken at a rest area behind the lines, not in the trenches, so we all look quite respectable and cheerful, the way people at home wanted soldiers to look. We'd all been de-loused and had our uniforms cleaned, and had a week without shelling or snipers. Quite a jolly little crew, aren't we? I was a lieutenant at the time, in charge of the platoon and I commissioned pictures of each section. I have copies of the pictures so you can do whatever you think fit with that one. Perhaps it will provide a reassuring memento for someone or other."

Emily studied the photograph. A group of a dozen monochromatic faces stared back at her, wide smiles frozen onto their faces. They were, as Kerry had said, all clean and fairly neat, beaming for the benefit of the camera. The captain himself stood behind them. He must have been raised up somehow, perhaps standing on a box or something similar. Except for the slight differences in uniform between lieutenant and captain – and they were very slight - he looked exactly the same. On the extreme right of the group, Emily recognised William Miller. He too was unchanged, with the same deceptively charming expression she remembered from her only meeting with him.

"I remember you saying you had never actually met Drake," said Kerry. "I can point him out to you..."

"There's no need, thank you. He's on the far left, as far away from Miller as he could get."

"Quite right. Had you seen pictures of him before, or had him described to you?"

"No, there's no need. He's the only one not wearing a cap."

Kerry laughed. "How did you know about that? It's typical of him. He always hated those uniform caps, I have no idea why. He even lost his a couple of times, which was a disciplinary offence though not a serious one. I suspect he lost them deliberately. In fact, it's the

139

only trouble I can remember him ever having been in. Overall, he was the most well-behaved soldier I've known."

Emily looked at the figure on the left of the group, wishing the reproduction was larger. The fair hair and open face with its wide smile was quite appealing in a boyish sort of way. Stephen Drake looked... she searched for the right word: amiable, approachable, playful even. According to Mary, she recalled, he'd had a fondness for tricks and practical jokes. She could see why he had attracted Mary. He was the kind of man who could never seem threatening or aggressive. She couldn't imagine him charging at the enemy with bayonet fixed and remembered Captain Kerry commenting during their first meeting that Drake hadn't been a particularly good soldier. It was true, the man with that face wouldn't have been.

"Thank you," she said out loud. "It's helpful to know just what he looked like."

"You're welcome to anything I can do, though I don't know what else there is under the circumstances. I'd better be going now and leave you to get on." He tossed the remains of the second cigarette into the fire and pushed himself upright with the aid of his walking stick. Emily caught sight of a brief involuntary grimace as he put weight onto his false leg, but carefully pretended not to have noticed it. Once upright, he hesitated before moving. His free hand went up to his face and the thumb and forefinger stroked his neat moustache. It was, she realised, an habitual gesture of which he was unconscious; no more than a nervous habit, something he did when he was unsure of himself. "There was something else, before I go..."

"Yes?"

"I know we've only met twice, and then for practical reasons, but I confess I've found our conversations interesting. This may be presumptuous of me but I wondered whether we could meet again, just

140

socially, with no particular purpose. I wondered, in fact, whether you would care to join me for lunch?"

Emily laughed out loud. "That's a very elaborate and apologetic invitation, captain. I'd be perfectly happy to join you for lunch, thank you, but not today I'm afraid. Today I shall be in Abbot's Sutton all day."

Kerry looked at her innocently. "Don't they serve lunch anywhere in Abbot's Sutton?"

"I'm sure they do, in fact I know they do. I've eaten there before."

"Even better," he said. "Then you know a good place for lunch."

"No. I know a place, but not a good one. I'm sure there must be better ones."

"Then you accept." He grinned at her triumphantly. "One o'clock? At Abbot's Sutton railway station?"

After he had left, Emily thought to herself in full awareness of the cliché, that life was full of surprises.

Chapter XV

Inspector Grice had a room of his own on the first floor of the police station. He always referred to it as his office, though in reality it was hardly more than a large cupboard with just enough space for a desk and two straight-backed chairs, providing the chairs were placed with their backs up against the walls. Nevertheless, it set him apart and emphasised the importance of his rank. Grice sat in one of the chairs and the other was currently occupied by Dr Pugh. The doctor had a stubby, short-stemmed pipe in his hands. He wasn't smoking it; he hardly ever did, but he constantly fiddled with it in his restless, impatient way. It was a habit that never failed to irritate Grice.

"So, have you progressed at all in determining the cause of death? Presumably there *was* a cause. The man didn't just keel over for no reason. He was an ex-soldier, looked fit enough. He didn't die of old age, did he?"

"Sarcasm," quoted Pugh, "is the lowest form of wit."

Grice glared at him. "You should choose your references more carefully. I believe the man who said that served two years in prison for gross indecency."

The doctor put his pipe in his mouth without bothering to light it, and retorted, "That says more about the laws you enforce than it does about the man." The belligerence of the response was rather spoiled by the fact that he found it difficult to enunciate with the pipe stem clenched between his teeth.

"Cause of death," repeated Grice firmly. "What was it?"

"I told you. Heart failure."

Grice took a deep breath and forced himself to be patient. "And what, may I ask, caused his heart to fail?"

"How should I know? I wasn't there. You don't want a doctor, you want a clairvoyant."

"Dr Pugh, please try to be more co-operative. I'm asking for a professional opinion to help me in my work."

"Well..." Reluctantly, Pugh relented a little. "The truth is, I don't know. I doubt anyone else would know either. A mystery, that's what it is. He seems a healthy man, as you say. I could cut him up, of course, just to check on that, but I don't imagine I'd find much wrong with him. There's no reason for a full autopsy as far as I can see. The man had a shock, something that was too much for his heart. We'll probably none of us ever know what it was, but there it is."

Grice leaned back in his chair. "It's not very satisfactory. My superiors aren't going to be pleased by that."

"That's your problem, not mine. If they want a second opinion, they're welcome to it."

"He wasn't attacked at all?"

The doctor took his pipe from his mouth and stared at it, as if inspiration may be lurking within its bowl. "Not in any way that left physical wounds. There are a few small bruises, mostly on his arms, but he could have got them when he assaulted Mary Calloway."

"*If* he assaulted Mary Calloway."

"All right, *if*. I suppose the law needs different standards of proof than the rest of us require. But Mary definitely fought back, you can see the signs of it on her own hands and arms. There was a struggle. Both of the bodies show evidence of it. There's nothing more than that on Miller, nothing that would have caused him any more than a bit of discomfort, let alone killed him."

Grice leaned forwards again and rested his elbows on the desk, frowning. "So what the hell happened up there?"

143

Pugh shrugged. "I wish I knew. You're not going to get a medical answer. Unless you unearth a witness, I doubt you'll ever find out."

"It's not good enough. Oh, I'm not blaming you..."

"You're not?" The doctor sounded surprised.

"No. You can be prickly, but you're competent enough."

"Thank you for that," said the doctor with heavy irony.

"I mean it. The thing is, I need something to report. I've got two bodies now. It's obvious enough what happened to Mary, but Miller... What about this frostbite on his hands? Is that what it turned out to be?"

"It is. And don't ask me to explain it, I can't."

"But there must *be* an explanation," persisted Grice. "There's an explanation for everything if you look hard enough. I know it wasn't cold enough up there in the night, but..."

Pugh interrupted him. "It's not just a question of the temperature. Look, I'll try to explain it to you. When it's cold – and I mean very, very cold – everything freezes; not just water, everything. As far as the human body is concerned, that means the muscles, the blood vessels, even the nerves. They all freeze. It's a nasty condition and it's very rare to see it as bad as Miller had it, but that's what happens. It affects the extremities first, the fingers and toes, then it can start to spread."

"That fits, certainly. It was Miller's fingers and hands that showed signs of it."

"Yes, but not his toes. That's odd to start with. The fact he was wearing shoes wouldn't explain it away. Ordinary shoes can't protect you against that degree of cold. But the most important thing is that the process of freezing takes time. Scott was in the Antarctic for months before frostbite set in. It's not something that happens overnight."

"Yet it does seem to have happened overnight, more or less."

144

"That is correct."

"And it definitely was frostbite."

"I've already said so, haven't I?"

"You have. And now you're telling me it's impossible."

"That is also correct."

Grice threw his hands in the air, exasperated. "What am I supposed to tell my superiors?"

"What am I supposed to tell the inquest? I suggest you say the same as I intend to. He had frostbite but it didn't kill him. With any luck nobody will be interested in any more than that."

"Luck? I don't like depending on luck."

Pugh stuffed his pipe into his coat pocket and grinned maliciously. "It's easy to tell you're not a doctor. We have to do it all the time. Well, if we're finished I have to go now. I have living patients to attend to and they're more important than dead ones. Also, they pay more."

"You're a cynical man, Dr Pugh."

"I'm a realist."

"I'll show you out."

The two men went down into the reception area, where Bert Lomas was manning the counter. The doctor left, and Grice paused to speak to Lomas. "Had any customers, constable? Anything I should know about?"

"Not much, sir. A lost purse, a complaint about offensive behaviour... the only one that might interest you is a woman who came in asking about Miller."

"Oh yes? Who was she?"

"She gave the name Duncan. She's not local, though I think I've seen her about the town a couple of times. A lady, I'd call her; very well dressed and well-spoken. Obviously comfortably placed, if you see what I mean, sir."

Interested now, Grice asked, "What did she want to know?"

"She wanted to know how Miller died, sir."

"Don't we all," said Grice with feeling. "I hope you threw her out on her ear."

Lomas stood up a little straighter, almost to attention. "I explained we couldn't divulge any information of that kind and advised her to wait for an official public statement." It was a careful little recitation, and when he had finished it he relaxed a little. "The truth is sir, I didn't think it was a good idea to offend anybody who dressed and spoke like she did."

"Christ," said Grice, "everybody's a bloody cynic today, even the young ones."

"Pardon, sir?" Lomas looked baffled.

"Oh, nothing. It doesn't matter."

"You're something of a dark horse, aren't you?" Kerry was sitting opposite Emily in the restaurant they had chosen after she met him at the station. The table was next to a window, with an inevitable view of the hills, though their peaks were now partially obscured by low cloud. They had finished their meal and were loitering at the table, talking. "You definitely gave me to understand that you were involved solely as a friend of Mary Calloway. Now I learn that you have entirely different motives for your interest."

His tone was mildly accusatory, but it was belied by a little half-smile.

"It's true, I did mislead you and I apologise for that. However, in my defence I didn't actually say anything untrue. At the time I believed the whole truth would have been too complicated and may have deterred you from talking to me at all."

"Oh, you don't need to apologise. You were probably right, but only because I hadn't met you then. As it turns out the whole truth is considerably more

146

interesting if not quite as altruistic. Are you sure it *is* the whole truth?"

Emily hesitated. "It is all of the truth that matters."

"Ah! A dark horse indeed. Well, we'll let that pass if you don't want to talk about it."

"I've only ever talked about it to one person and I'd rather it stayed that way. It's a personal matter."

Kerry nodded his assent without any further query, and took out his cigarettes. "Do you think anyone would object if I...?"

"I doubt it. There is an ashtray on the table, after all. And even if anyone did object they'd probably be too embarrassed to mention it; remember, you're a wounded war hero. You can do anything you like. Try it and see."

"Admirably pragmatic. I will." He lit the cigarette. "I must cut down on these now I no longer have the excuse of the war to justify myself. Tomorrow, perhaps."

Emily laughed. "I've heard that before, and I've no doubt I'll hear it again."

"I've no doubt you will. To return to the subject in hand, what made you tell me now?"

Emily thought about that, though in truth she had no need to think. She had worried the whole subject out beforehand. "There were two reasons. The first is that a little deception is acceptable; we all do it for both personal and social reasons, but I didn't feel justified in continuing it if we got to know one another better. That would have been a breach of trust."

"That's commendably honest of you. And the other reason?"

Emily smiled in an inadequate attempt to conceal her awkwardness. "Rather less commendable, I'm afraid. Quite selfish, in fact. I've spent the morning trying to discover exactly what happened to William Miller. I failed utterly. Most people know nothing and those who probably do know something – the police for example – refuse to talk to me. It's frustrating but perfectly understandable. In their eyes I'm simply an interfering woman indulging her morbid curiosity. I have no valid reason for asking, or no reason they would consider valid."

Kerry stared at her for a moment, then suddenly threw back his head and laughed out loud. "Whereas I, as Miller's company commander, would have a totally convincing reason. You're absolutely right. I'm sure if I limped into the police station playing the part of an officer and a gentleman they would take me into their confidence without hesitation. But you've forgotten something."

"I know. I haven't forgotten at all. You don't believe in ghosts, or in anything beyond the material. You told me as much. If that means you don't feel able to help me, I'll quite understand..."

"No, no. It's not that at all. I have no objection to the scientific study of so-called ghosts. In fact, I'm all in favour of it. Your work is deserving of support, as far as I am concerned. It has struck me in the past that the only people who object strongly to such enquiries are those who most passionately believe in ghosts. That's because they are afraid their cherished illusions will be exposed as falsehoods. We sceptics are perfectly happy for it all to be subject to scrutiny because we are confident we'll be proved right."

"But what if my investigations prove that ghosts do exist? How would you feel then?"

He shrugged. "That's academic. It won't happen. Ghosts don't exist so you can't possibly prove they do. *Quod erat demonstrandum*, as my old chemistry teacher used to say."

"You're very sure of yourself."

"On this particular subject, yes I am."

Arrogant about it, even, thought Emily. Instead she said, "So what is it I did forget?"

Kerry leaned forward onto the table. "If the police or anyone else tell me anything, they will undoubtedly specify that it is on condition that it remain confidential and that I tell no one else. So if I did learn anything about Miller's death, I wouldn't be able to tell you."

"I see. Yes, that's quite probable. What could we do about it?"

"Well, let me see..." He sat back, smoking his cigarette calmly. "I could tell you a story about a hypothetical man whose name most definitely wasn't Miller, and how this man died. That may be rather sophistical, but it may be enough to salve my conscience. Or on the other hand, we could take the path of expediency." He grinned at her unexpectedly. "You know, when we were on the front line there were occasional meetings with the top brass. They would ask us what morale was like, and all we company commanders would solemnly say, 'morale is first class, sir; very high'. We were lying, of course. How could morale possibly be high after four years of futile slaughter and squalor? We didn't look at each other because we all knew we were lying. The brass knew it as well. It was a kind of conspiracy. Everyone said what they were expected to say and nobody questioned it. It was understood. If any of us had told the truth about the condition of the men, or if any staff officer had openly doubted us, it would have upset the comfortable arrangement we all had. Reality would have reared its ugly head and no one would have known how to deal with it. The fiction had to be maintained, even though everyone recognised it for what it was."

Emily thought about this, then decided to make the implication explicit. "So you think that vows of confidentiality are the same sort of thing? Nobody really believes them, they're just saying what is expected of them?"

"Usually. It's like telling someone a secret and making them swear to keep it to themselves. You know perfectly well they're not going to. There's always someone they'll tell, and that person will tell someone else... You know how it works."

149

"So you'd lie?"

Kerry smiled at her and crushed out his cigarette. "How direct you can be. In short, yes."

Chapter XVI

"Frostbite?" Anthony Small was incredulous. "It wasn't nearly cold enough that night for even mild frostbite."

"That's what I said, and it appears everyone agrees. However, frostbite it was and by no means mild. Dr Pugh apparently described it as most severe. He even said that if Miller had lived, his hands would need to have been amputated."

"Good heavens!"

"Quite."

They sat in the vicarage study, comfortable and warm. The curtains were still open and outside white flakes were beginning to drift down again through the darkness, caught by the study lights as they floated past the window. The vicar's pipe was smouldering gently and Emily was consulting the notebook she had open on her lap.

"Well, Pugh is a competent doctor and a very down-to-earth man. He wouldn't have said anything so implausible if he wasn't certain of it."

"You know him, then?"

"Yes, we've known one another for some years. He's a non-conformist of course, and would never attend my church but that doesn't prevent us meeting every now and then. As a matter of fact, we play the occasional game of chess." The vicar smiled at some private recollections. "He's an excitable man, Dr Pugh, and his game is impulsive while mine is calculated. That means he usually loses, though the few games he does win tend to be spectacular and unpredictable victories. Professionally though, he's quite thorough. Perhaps when

I next see him I could ask whether his comments have been reported accurately. There is always the possibility of distortion when word passes from mouth to mouth."

"That would be helpful."

"But of course," Small went on, "he may not tell me. These things are usually meant to be confidential. Which leads me to ask, by the way, what is the source of your information?"

Emily closed her notebook and put it away, allowing herself time to think. Kerry had been very helpful when he need not have been. She did not want to get him into any trouble. On the other hand, she had already committed herself in no small measure to trusting the vicar. "I employed a spy," she admitted at last. "No one would talk to me, so I found someone they would be more likely to talk to."

"Someone they would talk to in confidence."

"Yes."

"And then he told you."

"Yes. We discussed it and agreed it would be acceptable for him to do that. You may think we were wrong."

It was the vicar's turn to allow himself time to think. He studied the bowl of his pipe, poked at it experimentally, decided it had gone out and laid it carefully on the arm of the chair. "No, I don't think so. One can be too fastidious in these matters. Confidentiality in such circumstances is rarely taken very seriously. One could just as easily condemn whoever gave your informant the information and say he shouldn't have done so. People will always talk, they can't resist it; and they always whisper that it's 'in confidence'."

"That's more or less what we decided."

"Just to satisfy my vulgar curiosity, may I ask who it was?"

Emily hesitated. "He's been very helpful to me. I wouldn't want to put him or anyone else into a difficult position."

The vicar carefully adjusted his spectacles and the corners of his mouth curled up in a sly smile. "In confidence, naturally."

"In *real* confidence?"

"You have my word on it."

"That's good enough. It was Captain Kerry."

"Ah, the young officer you visited in hospital. I remember. I had no idea you had kept in touch with him."

"I hadn't. He found me. He can be a very persistent young man."

"You were most impressed by him at your first meeting, as I recall."

"I was. I still am, in fact. He gave me this." She fished in her bag and produced the photograph. Small took it from her, then laid it on his lap while he took off and polished his glasses.

"Age," he explained. "One's eyesight suffers and I'm afraid I'm rather careless with the spectacles. Now, let me see..." He picked up the print and studied it. "Yes. That must be a platoon section judging by the number of men. I recognise Stephen Drake of course. And is that Miller on the other side? I've only seen the man a couple of times, but I believe it is. Fascinating. They all look so cheerful."

"It was taken behind the lines, at a rest centre."

"That explains it. And that must be your captain at the back. I see he had won a promotion since this picture was taken."

"Yes. He won a promotion and lost a leg. It hardly seems a fair exchange, does it?"

"Indeed not. He looks a very presentable young man."

"Is he? Yes, I suppose so. I hadn't taken much notice."

The vicar regarded her with mock-solemnity. "Now now, Miss Duncan. I've explained to you before that I can detect an untruth when I hear one."

Emily laughed ruefully. "So you have. Very well, yes, he is a presentable young man; quite handsome in a conventional sort of way. He also seems intelligent and unusually sensitive, which is far more important."

"It is, isn't it? An officer and a gentleman of the old school, in fact."

"Oddly enough, he used that very phrase himself earlier today, though he meant it ironically. It's true, nevertheless. Actually," Emily glanced up at the clock on the mantelpiece, "I'm to meet him at the station in an hour's time. I just wanted to drop in and speak to you first."

"I'm glad you did. An hour gives you plenty of time." The vicar unfolded his length from the chair and chose another pipe from the rack on his desk. While he was filling it from his tobacco jar, he went on talking. "So what do you make of this information elicited by your spy?"

"I don't know what to make of it. I gather no one else does either. The frostbite is the biggest puzzle, though apparently that wasn't what killed Miller. He died, I'm told, of heart failure following a shock of some kind."

The vicar laughed. "That sounds like a catch-all phrase, doesn't it? It says nothing and can't be contradicted. I'll wager that's something Dr Pugh comes out with when he can't think of anything else. As you say, the frostbite is the real conundrum. How would you explain it?"

"I wouldn't. That is to say, I can't. Can you?"

"Let me see..." He finished packing his pipe, drew on it to test it, then struck a match to light it. "Shall we experiment with a little hypothesis? Suppose Miller met Stephen Drake out on the hills."

"Drake, or his ghost?"

"Drake is dead, isn't he? You have your captain's word on that. So... ouch!" He abruptly dropped the match into the ashtray. While he was talking it had burnt down

154

unnoticed until it reached his fingers. He licked the fingers and struck another, this time lighting his pipe and disposing of the match before saying any more. "That's better. Where were we?"

Emily suppressed a smile. "We were supposing Miller met Drake."

"Exactly. Suppose he did. Now, when you originally interviewed Mary, I remember that you meticulously recorded the fact that she never touched him. That is correct, is it not?"

"It is. I made a point of ascertaining the fact."

"Why?" The vicar sat down again, the pipe in his mouth.

"Why?" Emily frowned. "Because I was trying to establish whether whatever Mary saw, whoever she spoke to, was materially present or not. You can see things that aren't there, you can even talk to people who aren't there, but it's most unusual to *touch* anything that isn't there. Touching is... inescapably physical. According to most accounts, whether true or not, it's actually impossible to touch a ghost. People talk about passing right through them as if they weren't there. Equally, ghosts are notoriously supposed to be able to pass through physical objects. Usually the walls of stately homes," she added with a smile, "a disproportionate number of ghosts being members of the aristocratic classes."

"You're correct, ghosts are popularly believed to be insubstantial." The vicar sat down again with his pipe finally alight to his satisfaction. "That's always been the case, as far back as ancient Rome. The *lemures* of the Romans were shades of the dead who restlessly roamed the earth in a way remarkably similar to our own ghosts, and they too were described as vague, shadowy beings; the spirits of those who had died violently or unexpectedly and without proper rites being observed. You could certainly say that about Stephen Drake, couldn't you?" He gazed round at the bookshelves,

155

speculatively. "St Augustine discusses the subject in his *'De Civitate Dei'* and I'm sure I remember a passage from Ovid... I must have it here somewhere..."

"Don't bother, I've read it," lied Emily hurriedly, forestalling what may have been a lengthy and ultimately futile search of the shelves. "What point were you making?"

"Point? Oh, yes. My point is that, as we've both said before, Stephen seems to be an unusually physical sort of ghost. According to tradition and received wisdom, one can't touch a ghost but... what would happen if one did?"

"I don't know." Emily was caught off-guard by the question. "I imagine it would be something of a shock, to say the least."

"Miller," Small pointed out placidly, "died of shock, as I understand it."

"So he did, but that doesn't necessarily mean...."

"It doesn't *necessarily* mean anything. If you recall, we were simply postulating a hypothesis. For some reason I've never understood, people always associate immortality with warmth; either the welcoming warmth of heaven or the somewhat less welcoming fires of hell. Perhaps they do so because death itself is so uncompromisingly cold that whatever comes after must be differentiated from it as firmly as possible. Have you ever touched a dead body?"

"Yes. My mother's."

"Well, I've touched many in the course of my work and I find the overwhelmingly strong impression one gets is always that of how cold they are."

"Yes," said Emily reluctantly. "That's true."

"I'm sorry if I'm upsetting you but it may be important."

"Carry on. You're not upsetting me." It was another lie.

"Touching a ghost must be the closest anyone can get to touching death itself, and death is very, very cold

156

indeed. Cold enough, perhaps, to freeze the skin, the blood vessels, the nerves... everything."

"What a horrible thought."

"Yes, isn't it?" The vicar looked perfectly calm, sitting back in his armchair with his long legs crossed at the knee and his pipe in his hand. He could equally well have been discussing the weather or the timing of the next choir practice. "That's what frostbite is."

"But..." Emily paused, frantically following a train of thought. "Are you suggesting...?"

"I'm not suggesting anything. At least, I'm not saying that anything specific actually happened. But we have a phenomenon that appears to have no explanation at all, so we may need to fall back upon what you once described to me as your explanation of last resort. If we do, then I say that explanation may at least carry some theoretical conviction. That is the most I will say."

"But it doesn't," objected Emily. "There is still the time factor to be accounted for. Frostbite takes a long time to reach the stage at which Miller had it. Even if he had been exposed to the most extreme cold, there wasn't enough time for it to have had the effect it did."

"Come now, Miss Duncan. If we are willing to entertain the possibility that temperature may be different in the presence of death, surely we shouldn't cavil at the idea that the passage of time may also differ. That, after all, is a commonplace in accounts of the supernatural. If the dead experience time at all, there is no reason to assume that they experience it as the living do; there would be every reason to doubt it, in fact. And those in physical contact with the dead may share in that distortion of time."

Emily thought for a while, then took out her notebook and began to write. After only a few words, though, she stopped. "This is no good. There are no facts for me to record. It's all sheer fantasy. You're speculating on no grounds whatsoever. There's no empirical evidence, only metaphysical conjecture."

"There is evidence," the vicar corrected her gently. "Not, admittedly, evidence for my little hypothesis but evidence that must be explained somehow. There is Miller's body and Dr Pugh's account of it. That's hard evidence and it can't be ignored. I confess I have been a little... shall we say, imaginative? Yes, imaginative in my explanation but I can't produce a better one. If you can, I shall be most pleased to hear it."

Emily looked from his relaxed figure in the armchair to her notebook, then back again. "I'll think about it," she said.

The vicar smiled benignly. "Do."

There were few people about as Emily walked down from the vicarage to the station. The snow was falling steadily, large flakes floating down in still air, but it had only just begun to settle on the road and pavements; a thin film of white, still semi-transparent over the dark ground. On the hills, it would be a thicker, more opaque covering. Captain Kerry was waiting for her on the platform. The station lamps had been lit and she saw him immediately as she walked through the gates. There was hardly anyone else there, only a handful of patient passengers and a bored porter leaning against his trolley. Kerry was standing upright under the shelter of the canopy beneath one of the lamps, resting both hands on the walking stick he held in front of him. Emily was momentarily startled by how military he looked, with his uniform and his erect stance, as if he were at attention on parade. It was difficult to make any connection with the man she had talked to over lunch, he looked too severe and unapproachable, rendered somehow anonymous by his uniform and his posture. As she approached, he saw her and visibly relaxed; the brief illusion was shattered. He stepped towards her and another illusion was broken. When he had been standing still it would have been impossible to tell there was anything wrong with his leg, but once he moved the awkward limp became obvious. He must be tired, she thought suddenly. He'd done too much walking on the new leg, which still gave him some discomfort. She felt guilty because, influenced by his own insouciance, she had failed to take that into account. She had been too absorbed by her own preoccupations: selfish in fact, not to put too fine a point on it.

They found a compartment to themselves, which was not difficult at that time of day, and settled into seats facing one another. No other arrangement even occurred to either of them.

"You don't object to having your back to the engine?"

He laughed. "Not in the least. I've travelled in cattle trucks before now, and worse than that. I don't mind which direction I'm facing as long as I have a comfortable seat. How did you get on with your vicar?"

"Oh, he's a good man. Mary Calloway once described him as 'a decent old chap' and in a way that sums it up, though he's actually more perceptive than such a phrase would lead one to believe. Or that his own appearance would lead one to believe, come to that. I must say, though, that today he seemed to me to be talking nonsense; well, perhaps not nonsense exactly but certainly going far beyond what could be justified by the facts."

"You mustn't hold that against him. Talking nonsense occasionally is an occupational hazard for a clergyman. You should have heard some of the army chaplains. They were decent chaps too, for the most part, but when they started trying to explain how a benevolent God could allow the carnage we all had to live with..." He shook his head. "Sometimes it was difficult trying to keep a straight face – or trying to keep one's temper, depending on how seriously one took it."

159

"And how seriously did you take it?"

"Not very. The whole thing was so obviously unjustifiable that I took little notice of anyone who tried. They had to do it, it was part of their job. But I didn't have to listen to them."

"There's something I've often wondered when men talk about the front. Tell me, if you have no objection, if you felt like that about it why did you enlist in the first place?"

"Like everyone else, I had no idea what it would be like. We were innocents, all of us. If I'd known then..." He tailed off into silence.

"You wouldn't have joined up?" Emily prompted him.

"I honestly don't know. That's the easy answer, but perhaps I would have after all. It's all more complicated than it ought to be, and of course once you're there you have to carry on. You owe it to the rest of the men. Also," he grinned suddenly, "they shoot you if you don't. That's a wonderful incentive. Besides, if I hadn't enlisted I'd eventually have been called up so it makes little difference."

Make light of it, Emily thought. They all do it. The casual dismissal, sometimes the gallows humour. Perhaps that was the only way most people had of coping with such an awful reality.

"So," Kerry changed the subject, "despite my sleuthing on your behalf, you're no further forward with your enquiries?"

"I'm more confused than ever," Emily admitted. "I've never come across a case like this before. It makes no sense at all. Even so, thank you for your help. I appreciate it."

"Good. I did rather go out of my way to assist you, didn't I?"

"You did." Emily was cautious, sensing that this uncharacteristic remark was leading somewhere.

"Do you think I deserve a favour in return?"

160

"That depends on what it is."

"Yes. Well, I had been rather hoping that our lunch today would be a purely social occasion; nothing to do with wars or ghosts or anything like that, just ordinary life. You know, chatting about the weather, getting to know one another better, that sort of thing. However, that's not how it turned out. My idea is that perhaps we could try it again?"

He was stroking his moustache again, that absent movement of thumb and forefinger that Emily had already identified as a symptom of nervousness.

"Perhaps we could."

"Excellent! How about dinner tonight, perhaps at your hotel as it's so much better than mine?"

"Captain..."

"You do owe me a favour, you said so yourself."

"I did, but..."

"That's settled then. It's quite a small favour, after all. Who knows, you may even enjoy it. What time shall I call on you?"

"Captain," Emily repeated firmly. "I may be jumping to the wrong conclusion. If so, I hope you'll forgive me. But may I ask, how old are you?"

"I'm twenty seven. Why?"

"Because I am forty, or as near forty as makes no difference."

"You don't look it."

"Don't be silly. In common with most women, I spend enough time in front of the mirror every morning to know exactly what I look like. There are many women in this country at the moment, legions of women in fact, who are of Mary Calloway's age and whose young men haven't returned from the war. Don't you think your time would be better spent with one of them instead of with a middle-aged woman who has an eccentric hobby?"

"No." His response was immediate and uncompromisingly obstinate. He had an odd way of tilting his head back which made his chin jut out and emphasised his intractability It was a mannerism Emily had never seen in him before, but it must have been familiar to his soldiers and probably to his superiors. "I think my time would be best spent with someone I find interesting."

Emily sighed. "You can be a most persistent young man."

Kerry's face wore the little half-smile she remembered from their first meeting. "Persistent? I think I prefer 'persevering'. They mean the same, but 'persistent' somehow sounds like a criticism whereas 'persevering' is definitely a compliment. Also, you haven't answered my question; what time shall I call on you?"

"I believe I'll keep to 'persistent' if it's all the same to you."

"What time? Shall we say seven thirty?"

Emily smiled despite herself. "Very well, let it be seven thirty."

"Good." He settled back in his seat. "Do you mind if I smoke?"

"I've already told you not to bother asking."

"So you have. I'd forgotten."

Chapter XVII

The weather was not too bad for Mary Calloway's funeral the following day. The snow had stopped, although there was still a covering on the ground, hardly more than a layer of white dust. Unexpectedly a thin, watery sun also showed its face for the duration of the actual burial. The Reverend Small had officiated at many funerals since his ordination and he was fully aware of the effect that something as basic as the weather could have on the atmosphere of the proceedings. Doctrine and faith were all very well, but they paled into insignificance in the face of heavy rain, intense cold or snow. The worse the weather, the more difficult people found it to believe in the immortality of the soul and the promise of the life to come. There was no logic to it of course, but in the presence of intense emotion logic had little relevance; less, even, than the weather.

In the weak sunlight, the gathered mourners were sombre but not despairing. The Calloway family stood as a little group apart, next to the open grave. They were isolated in the same way they had been in their pews during the memorial service. Perhaps it was because others were unwilling to intrude upon the privacy of their grief; or perhaps, less charitably, it was because people instinctively regarded grief as something to be kept at a safe distance in case it were somehow contagious. They appeared, the Reverend Small thought, mysteriously reduced, diminished. The bereaved often had that look, as if something had been taken out of them leaving them shrunken, subdued. And in a way, of course, it had. Mrs Calloway, in particular, was worryingly frail; so much so that the vicar made a mental note to talk to her doctor.

She seemed to have lost weight even in the few days that had passed. She was gaunt, haggard, an ill woman. Her husband looked much as he usually did except that he was standing unnaturally still, a lifeless waxwork imitation of himself.

As he intoned the words from the Book of Common Prayer, which he knew by heart, the Reverend Small found his gaze wandering around the mourners and beyond them, probing the far corners of the churchyard, searching amongst the headstones and monuments. He looked even into the trees that crowded in upon the graveyard walls. His mind was elsewhere, though his voice continued automatically.

"Man that is born of a woman hath but a short time to live, and is full of misery. He cometh up, and is cut down, like a flower; he fleeth as it were a shadow, and never continueth in one stay."

What was he looking for? He knew perfectly well what it was, though he would never have admitted it to anyone present. His visual search was discreet so as not to offend, not to interrupt the ritual nor to impinge upon the grief of those in attendance.

"Forasmuch as it hath pleased Almighty God of his great mercy to take unto himself the soul of our dear sister here departed: we therefore commit her body to the ground; earth to earth, ashes to ashes, dust to dust."

What he was half-expecting to see was a bare-headed, fair-haired figure in army uniform. He thought he may glimpse it somewhere in the shadows, somewhere outside the little huddle of figures around the grave.

But there was nothing to be seen.

"It was a most pleasant evening," said Emily. "I enjoyed myself. You can be good company once we escape the usual subjects."

"Thank you. I also enjoyed it. My persistence justified itself in the end, then?"

"Your perseverance," Emily corrected him, "was fully justified."

They both laughed, something they had done many times during and after their dinner engagement. They occupied a bench on the platform of Ludlow station, a much larger and busier affair than that of Abbot's Sutton. Kerry had insisted on seeing her off even though she pointed out that it was completely unnecessary for what was no more than a fifteen minute journey, and that she would be back within a few hours.

"I must," he had protested. "I have to return to my unit soon, after which I may not see you for some time. At least allow me the pleasure of your company as much as possible before I go."

"Do you really have to return?" she asked him now, as they sat waiting for the train. "Haven't you already done enough? What can be the point of going back?"

"It's a formality, I've no doubt. After all, I'm not of much use to them now but until my discharge comes through I'm still subject to army discipline. I have to show my face for a while."

"I haven't asked, but what do you intend to do after your discharge?"

"I've really no idea. I have no private means, so I suppose I'll have to find a job. That won't be the easiest task in the world, with several hundred thousand men all suddenly in need of jobs all within a few months."

"What did you do before the war?"

165

"I worked as a clerk in a merchant bank. It was unimaginably tedious and I have no desire to return to it. In fact, I suspect the desire to escape from it was instrumental in my decision to enlist in the first place. Fool that I was, I thought a taste of adventure would be an exciting change. Besides, they haven't kept my job open for me. I can't really blame them for that; commerce goes on, war or no war, and they had to have someone to deal with it. Their transactions couldn't all be put on hold for four years."

They sat for a while in silence, then Emily said, "Even so, a man like yourself should be able to find something..."

"A man like myself? Remember what I am, Miss Duncan."

"You're educated, intelligent, with a good war record..."

"So are many men. The features that distinguish me from the others are that I'm a cripple with no particular qualifications. I'm not feeling sorry for myself, but one must face up to these things. As a matter of fact, I've been meaning to talk to you about it but I didn't know how to introduce the subject. I didn't want to appear to be asking for sympathy. Nothing could be further from my mind."

"Then why did you want to talk to me about it? I don't understand."

"Don't you?" The curious half-smile was on his face again.

"No."

"The point is, if we're going to continue our association after my discharge you shouldn't be under any illusions about my prospects."

"I can't imagine why. Your prospects would only have any relevance to our acquaintance under very particular circumstances and those circumstances don't apply. Unless, that is, you are attempting an indirect proposal of marriage?"

166

"Certainly not!" The half-smile transformed into an open grin. "We haven't known one another long enough. Yet," he added as an afterthought.

"Don't be so foolish. But if we are to see one another when your army career is over..."

"I hope so."

"*If* we are, then I won't be able to go on calling you 'captain', will I? I don't believe captains can carry on using their rank after their service is over."

"You're quite right, we're not nearly elevated enough. I wouldn't want to anyway; it would be a constant reminder of something I'd prefer to forget. My name is Robert."

"I know. I looked you up before our first meeting; background research. Do your friends call you Bob?"

"No. Not if they wish to remain my friends."

"Very well, Robert it is. My name is Emily."

"Really? Somehow you don't look like an Emily. It's not sufficiently sophisticated. I imagined something of French origin, to match your elegant clothes."

"Nevertheless, that's what it is. It's derived from the Latin Aemilia, a patrician name which ought to be sophisticated enough for anyone. If you don't like it, you can carry on calling me Miss Duncan."

"I do like it," he reassured her. "I'm just being tactless, as ever. And just on time to cover my embarrassment, I believe this must be your train."

The engine pulled into the station amidst a cloud of steam and the accompanying noises of mechanical pressure being released, trailing half a dozen passenger carriages. Emily stood up and Kerry, with some slight difficulty, immediately joined her.

"So it is. Well, I'm sure I'll see you again, Robert. *Before* you rejoin your regiment. As for afterwards... we'll see. No doubt you still have my card."

"I do." Kerry patted the breast pocket of his tunic with an expression of mock-solemnity. "Naturally I keep it always next to my heart."

167

"Idiot!"

In her compartment after boarding the train, Emily thought about the conversation and suddenly, on impulse, threw back her head and laughed out loud. The only other occupant of the compartment, a pink and portly young man with a travelling salesman's case of samples on the seat beside him, looked startled and hid behind a newspaper to cover either confusion or disapproval, it was impossible to tell which. That made Emily laugh again, though this time she tried unsuccessfully to stifle it. It was not, after all, appropriate behaviour for a respectable middle-aged woman in a public place.

The main street of Abbot's Sutton had become very familiar since her first visit. Then, everything had been strange. Now every building, every shop was known to her. She recognised them all, had been inside many of them. One or two people even smiled and nodded to her in the street as they passed. They had seen her before, she was no longer a total stranger. Some of them had faces that were known to her. There was the polite but impossibly young constable she had seen in the police station; the even younger postman who had first directed her to the Calloway's house; a nervous girl who had served her lunch in an over-polite restaurant. The 'Calloway and sons' delivery van was once more parked outside the grocer's, marking the primacy of commerce over personal grief. Business went on. It occurred to Emily that she was even wearing the same coat she had worn on her first visit, the Burberry gabardine with its fur collar that Mary had admired so much. That was the trouble with staying away from home; one's wardrobe became necessarily limited.

Then, as she approached the top of the street, the most familiar face of all. The vicar was emerging from

168

the tobacconist's shop, tucking his purchase into the pocket of his shabby old coat. He saw her and his long face broke into a welcoming smile.

"Miss Duncan, this is a surprise. I was beginning to think I wouldn't see you again."

"I was here the day before yesterday, that's hardly a long absence."

"No. No, of course not. It's just that, with all that's happened... Well, to be honest I wondered if you had abandoned your investigation."

"I almost have," Emily admitted, "I can't see any way to continue it, and it has become distasteful to me in any case, but I would have called to say goodbye regardless. Mary's funeral was yesterday, wasn't it?"

"It was. A sad affair naturally, but they always are."

"I stayed away deliberately. I thought my presence may be an unwelcome reminder of things the family would prefer to forget."

"I understand that. I didn't expect to see you there. Though none of it was your fault in any way, I hope you appreciate that fact."

"You're right, it wasn't. However, that unfortunate newspaper article was what brought me and it was also what brought Miller. It was, indirectly, the cause of Mary's death. I can't avoid a feeling of... not of responsibility, which would be unjustified, but of a kind of guilt by association. It's more emotion than logic, I freely admit, but I think it may be an emotion Mr and Mrs Calloway would have shared. I didn't want to add to their troubles."

"Very commendable. I believe you made the right decision."

Emily hesitated, then said, "I suppose there weren't any... unexpected mourners at the funeral?"

"No." The vicar smiled at her, rather sadly, she thought. "I looked for him, but he wasn't there."

"Ah well. What a pity. It would have been... appropriate. Who would have had a greater right to be there?"

"Nobody at all. But living or dead, he wasn't."

"I thought, having missed the funeral, that while I'm here I may visit Mary's grave. Do you think that would be acceptable?"

"Certainly. I'll walk with you as far as the church, if you'll permit me."

They continued up the street, the vicar moderating his lanky stride to keep pace with Emily. The church tower loomed ahead of them, square and uncompromisingly ecclesiastical, rising above the busy little town. Beyond it were the hills, higher still and much, much older. There was perhaps, Emily thought, some symbolism in that if one had a mind for such things. At the churchyard gates, they paused.

"I have some business to attend to," said the Reverend Small. "It shouldn't take long. The grave is over by the wall, in that direction." He pointed in the direction of the hills. "There's no headstone yet, it's still being carved, but even so you can't miss it. It's the only recent one in that area."

"I'll find it, thank you."

"When I've finished, I'll look for you. If you're still there, perhaps we could go to the vicarage and share what may be our last cup of Mrs Claypole's tea?"

"That would be very welcome."

Left alone, Emily walked in the direction the vicar had indicated, picking her way amongst the graves and monuments. She was moving towards the trees. On the other side of the wall was the path from which Mary had emerged for their second and last meeting. On the other side of the path was the little wooded area where she'd had her only encounter with William Miller. It was familiarity again, just as in the town. They were places she knew, physical reminders of people she had known, however briefly, and who were now dead.

170

The grave, as the vicar had promised, was impossible to miss. That was not solely because the earth was newly turned and the flowers were fresh. It was also because there was someone standing at the foot of it, staring down; a man in soldier's uniform but bare-headed. Emily stopped in her tracks. She felt suddenly, unaccountably faint as if the blood had drained from her head. Her conscious mind was empty, refusing to accept what her eyes saw. It took a supreme effort for her to make her feet move and slowly approach the figure. As she came closer, he turned and smiled at her.

She recognised him at once, from the photograph Kerry had given her.

Chapter XVIII

"Hello." His smile was open, engagingly innocent. His voice was soft and warm, with only a trace of the local accent. The fair hair was fine and unruly, like a boy's. He looked out of place in uniform, almost as if he were dressed up to play a part. Emily heard Captain Kerry's voice in the back of her mind saying, 'he wasn't a particularly good soldier. He was too... *nice*, if you know what I mean'. Not Captain Kerry now, of course, or not for much longer. Robert Kerry. She tried to force herself to banish irrelevancies and concentrate on the figure before her.

"Hello. You must be Stephen Drake."

"That's right." The smile widened. "It seems my reputation precedes me."

"It does." Her voice was trembling. She must stop that happening. With an enormous effort of will she forced herself to move closer to Drake, until she was standing no more than a couple of feet away from him. "I wasn't at Mary's funeral," she said, "but I wanted to pay my respects."

"Likewise." He seemed completely at ease, carrying on a normal, polite conversation in that quiet, mellifluous voice he had. "To tell you the truth, I thought my presence at the funeral might cause some consternation. That's why I stayed away. I didn't want to be a distraction."

"No, of course you didn't. It would have been quite a distraction though, wouldn't it? Something of a sensation, in fact."

"I'm afraid so." He sounded genuinely regretful.

172

This was ridiculous. One couldn't exchange pleasantries with a dead man. Something had to be said.

"Tell me," asked Emily in a voice she couldn't prevent from shaking, "Are you my first ghost?"

He tilted his head to one side, considering the question. "I don't know. Am I?"

"That depends on whether you really are a ghost or not. I've never seen one before so if you are, you're my first."

"I don't feel much like a ghost, but then I don't know how a ghost ought to feel. It's something of a conundrum, isn't it?"

"I've spoken to Captain Kerry. He says he saw you killed, with no possibility of mistake."

"If he said that, you can be sure he meant it. He's a decent sort, the captain, despite being an officer. I'd quite like to see him again myself, if it were possible."

"I doubt he'd be amenable. He doesn't believe in ghosts."

"No, I should think not. He always was a sensible fellow. And if I wasn't a ghost, he'd have to arrest me for desertion and I don't suppose he'd enjoy that much, either."

This was getting nowhere. To her own surprise, Emily discovered her nervousness was evaporating. Drake was a very easy man to talk to. She could easily see why Mary Calloway had liked him. "You're very adept at avoiding questions," she told him. "You should have been a politician."

He laughed. "I assume that's not meant to be a compliment. I don't really avoid questions. It's just that I rarely know any answers and one has to say something, doesn't one?"

"Are you dead?" Emily asked him directly. "Yes or no, please."

"If Captain Kerry says I am, then I must be."

"That's neither yes nor no."

"You ask very difficult questions. A simple yes or no doesn't always cover all the possibilities."

"I'd have thought it would in this case."

"No. That's not 'No, I'm not dead', it's 'No, it doesn't cover all the possibilities'. Sorry for any ambiguity."

"It's all ambiguity," said Emily.

"Life's like that. So is death, perhaps."

"You know, you can be infuriating."

He laughed again. "Mary always used to say that, particularly when I teased her. Poor Mary."

They both spontaneously looked down at the freshly-filled grave and the floral tributes scattered over it. Poor Mary, indeed.

"Mary's dead," said Emily. "That, at least, is certain."

"I'm afraid so. She was too trusting. She was completely taken in by Miller. I warned her against him, you know. That was all I could do. But he could be deceptively convincing, especially when he was dealing with women."

"Yes, I know. Do you think," she asked abruptly, "that you'll see her again?"

"How can I?" He looked blank, uncomprehending. "She's dead."

"So are you, aren't you? I meant in the afterlife."

"In heaven, you mean? I doubt it. I've never truly believed in heaven, it's too much like wishful thinking. Don't tell the vicar that though, will you? It would upset him."

Emily closed her eyes for a moment to gather her thoughts, then quickly opened them again in case Drake had disappeared, but he was still there as solid and physical as before. She saw now what Mary had meant about the almost unnatural physicality of him, the texture of the rough serge uniform and polished leather belt and brass buttons. He appeared somehow more real or more distinct than anyone she had ever seen.

174

"How does it feel," she asked, "being dead? I feel stupid asking such a question but it's one everybody has wanted answered for millennia."

"I don't have an answer, I'm afraid. You say I'm dead. Captain Kerry says I'm dead. The fact is, I don't feel much different from how I always felt. A little vague, perhaps. There are things I don't remember, especially about that last little skirmish and coming back from France; things that seem... confused. My memory has always been good, but now there seem to be blank patches in it. It's like watching a play where you skip from scene to scene. You know things happen in between the scenes, but you never actually experience them. But I'm still the same person I always was."

"And why are you here? I don't mean at the grave, I mean here in this town and in the hills."

"It's home," he answered simply. "And I came back to see Mary. Now she's gone, I doubt I'll stay long."

"What will happen to you afterwards?"

"None of us knows that, do we?"

"I thought in your position you may have some special insight."

"No." He grinned. "I've never been renowned for my insight and as I said – I'm still the same person. I just feel somehow that I won't be around here for much longer. I'm like someone in a waiting room, expecting my train to turn up. I don't know where it's going, but I'm sure it will be here soon."

Emily studied him. It was impossible to believe he was in any way unreal. "tell me something else," she said suddenly, "why don't you ever wear your uniform cap?"

"My cap?" He laughed again. It was something he did often, an open, unself-conscious laugh. "What an odd question. I always hated the things. They're hardly the height of sartorial elegance, are they? And so impractical. I was always leaving mine lying about, not deliberately if you see what I mean, but half-hoping it would never turn up again. I got into trouble for it once."

175

"Yes, so Captain Kerry told me."

"Did he? Fancy him remembering that, of all things. It always did turn up, of course. I expect it will again, unfortunately."

"Don't you get cold in this weather, without your cap or coat?"

"No. The temperature doesn't seem to affect me the way it used to. I hardly notice it at all, to tell you the truth. Time, temperature... *I* haven't changed but the world around me seems to have changed. Odd, isn't it?"

"Yes. Perhaps that's what it's like, being a ghost."

"Perhaps it is. If so, it's not how I ever imagined it."

"Nor I. May I ask you something else?"

"Anything you like, though I may not be able to answer it."

Emily took one step closer to him, suddenly nervous again. "Can I touch you?"

"Touch me?" He considered, then said slowly, "You *can*, though I wouldn't recommend it. Not a good idea at all, in fact. The results are unpredictable, you see."

"Is that what happened to Miller? Did he try to touch you?"

"He tried to strangle me." Drake's voice didn't change. It was still quiet, casual, conversational. "I advised him not to, but he took no notice. I didn't do anything to him, you understand. I didn't need to, he did it to himself. Violence was always Bill Miller's answer to anything, always his first response. Whenever anyone crossed him or he couldn't get what he wanted, he'd immediately turn violent. Rather like a spoilt child, you could say; but a dangerous, grown-up one. Mary found that out." He looked sadly down at the grave. "Anyway, our little chat has been interesting but I'm afraid I must be on my way now. I doubt we'll meet again." He grinned at her. "And I'll avoid shaking your hand in case of unintended consequences."

176

"Do you really have to leave? I have so much to ask you."

"I really do. I have... my train to catch, so to speak."

"What happens? Do I close my eyes and you mysteriously disappear?"

"That little trick? Did Mary tell you about that?"

"Yes, she did."

"I used to enjoy playing tricks on her. It was wicked of me, I suppose, but I think she enjoyed it too."

"How did you do it?"

He shrugged. "Oh, I don't know. It wasn't a trick at all really. It just happens when I want it to, I can't claim any credit for cleverness or anything like that. Would you like me to do it again?"

"No, I don't think I would, thank you. You can just walk away like anyone else."

"Is that so that you can follow me? Do you want to know where I'm going?"

"I'd dearly love to know where you're going but I don't think I'd be brave enough to follow you."

He laughed. "A good answer. However, I believe I may have to disappear after all. We're no longer alone."

He was looking over her shoulder. Emily instinctively turned and saw the Reverend Small picking his ungainly way amongst the gravestones. When she turned back again, predictably, the man who had been standing hardly a foot away from her had vanished. She felt deflated, disappointed. Then, in reaction, she began to tremble uncontrollably. She had not been frightened all the way through the conversation, it had all been too normal, too ordinary for that, and Drake had been too polite and friendly; a nice man, as everyone agreed. But now that it was over she was suddenly overwhelmed by the knowledge that she had been talking with a dead man – just as her mother had once done. Was it the same thing? Could it even possibly be the same?

177

"Sorry I'm late," said the vicar as he approached her. "I was delayed for longer than expected. Still, I noticed you'd found someone to talk to which must have helped pass the time. Where has he gone, by the way? Was it anyone I'd know?"

"I haven't the faintest glimmer of an idea where he's gone; and yes, it was someone you'd know."

The vicar looked around him, then looked back at her. "I see. Yes, I thought he was in uniform but that's still not uncommon. It never occurred to me..." He looked more closely. "Good heavens, you don't appear at all well. Your face is unnaturally pale. Are you ill? It's not a return of your influenza, I hope."

Emily managed a weak laugh. "One question at a time, please! No, it's not influenza. It's a reaction of some sort but I do feel rather weak."

"You look it. Can you manage the walk to the vicarage? I'll assist you, if you'll allow me."

"There's no need. I can walk." Emily turned, but the vicar had paused and was looking down at Mary's grave.

"Well, well. What have we here?"

With some trepidation, Emily followed his gaze. She didn't know what she was about to see, and didn't want to see anything out of the ordinary. In a way, it wasn't particularly out of the ordinary though it was admittedly out of place. There was a military cap lying on the grave amongst the flowers.

"How very odd," he said pensively. "How did that get there? It looks like another tribute, though an unconventional one."

"It wasn't there last time I looked," Emily told him.

The vicar bent down to pick it up.

"No, don't touch it!" cried Emily urgently. She was suddenly, irrationally, afraid.

The vicar smiled at her. "Why not? It's only a military cap like millions of others." Deliberately he took

178

it in his hands and held it up. Nothing else happened and Emily realised she had been holding her breath. She let it out with an enormous, audible sigh of relief. The vicar studied the badge. "I'm no expert, but I believe that's the right regiment. I've seen a few of these badges over the past four years and one gets to recognise them." He turned the cap over in his hands and inspected the inside. Wordlessly, he showed it to her. Attached to the inner band were a small number of short, fair hairs.

"Would you like to keep it?" he asked. "It may constitute evidence of a sort for your investigation."

"No." Emily didn't even want to touch it. It wasn't any kind of revulsion, or even fear. It was more a feeling of sensibility, of appropriateness, of simple decorum even. "No, I think it belongs where it was put by its owner."

"Quite right. That was my thought exactly, but I wondered if you would disagree in the name of scientific enquiry."

"No."

"Good." Carefully, he replaced the cap in precisely the position from which he had lifted it. "Now, we were talking earlier about tea at the vicarage but given your state of nerves, I think we would be justified in making it a restorative glass of sherry."

Chapter XIX

Habit establishes itself remarkably quickly. Emily had been in the Reverend Small's study less than half a dozen times yet it was already a haven of secure familiarity, emotionally comforting and calming. Emily automatically occupied the same seat as she had on the first occasion, and waited in silence while the vicar went through the rituals of pouring sherry then filling and lighting the pipe he selected from his rack. He took his time and she felt no impatience. Eventually, he sank back into his chair and stretched out his long legs, glass in his hand and the sweet smoke from his pipe scenting the air.

"So, it's finally happened," he said. "You've seen a ghost."

"Yes, and spoken to him."

"But not touched him?"

"No." She gave a little smile. "I thought it would be... unwise. He warned me against it."

"I wonder if he also warned Miller."

"He says he did. I believed him. He seemed a very honest sort of ghost."

"It's odd, isn't it? One always thinks of ghosts and apparitions as 'it', yet you talk about 'him'."

"That's because he was very human as well as being honest. When you've stood talking to a man, discussing things with him, you can't refer to him as 'it'. That would be unnatural."

"Unnatural. Yes. Some would say the entire thing was unnatural. You may have said as much yourself not so very long ago."

Emily sipped her sherry. Like the room itself, the drink was warm and comforting. "I would still say it.

That was what unnerved me, especially after it was over and I started thinking about it. At the time... I won't claim it was a perfectly normal conversation but it was really quite ordinary apart from the subject matter."

"And what was the subject matter?"

"We talked about Mary, of course. Also about Miller. You were perfectly right about what happened to Miller, by the way. Drake said Miller attacked him, tried to strangle him. He didn't say why. He didn't seem to think it required any explanation other than Miller's character." Emily sipped her sherry and tried to recall what else had been said at the graveside. It was surprisingly difficult considering the whole episode had been only a matter of minutes ago. "We also talked about abstract things. I remember asking him a lot of questions but I don't remember many direct answers. He was very vague, deliberately so, I thought. He did say his perception of time and temperature had changed."

"That's hardly surprising."

"No. Other than that, what he said was mainly that he was the same person he had always been, that he didn't feel much different from when he was alive."

"So he did actually admit that he was dead?"

Emily thought about it then shook her head. "No. No, he didn't. That's me putting words into his mouth, I'm afraid. *I* said it several times and he never disagreed but I don't recall him ever actually saying it himself. Why?"

The vicar shrugged and concentrated on his pipe, which he had neglected and was threatening to go out.

"He wasn't at all ghostly," said Emily. "That was my first reaction when I heard Mary's account, and the way she described him fits perfectly. I felt the same. It was as if I'd just met someone casually and had a polite conversation. Of course, I didn't know him when he was alive so I can't vouch for him being unchanged, but he was certainly very physical; an ordinary man standing beside a grave."

181

"Leaving behind him," the vicar pointed out, "an ordinary cap on the ground. An eminently physical cap with no mysterious qualities."

"Except for the fact that it wasn't there earlier."

"So you say, and I don't doubt you for a moment. But Stephen Drake was very fond of what he called his 'tricks'. Making things appear and disappear was amongst them."

"Yes, he mentioned that himself." Emily frowned. "Do I understand you correctly? After all this, are you suggesting Stephen Drake is still alive after all, and that I have just been talking to him?"

"You've certainly just been talking to him, whether living or dead."

"But..." Emily paused then burst out irritably, "I should have taken notes. If only I could remember exactly what he said..."

"I'm sure you had other things on your mind than the taking of notes."

"I shouldn't have had." Emily was vehement, annoyed with herself. "That's what I do. I study and I take notes."

The Reverend Small smiled benignly, his pipe now alight again to his satisfaction. "You are a human being as well as a scientist. You failed to take notes because of the emotional importance of what was happening to you. That's perfectly understandable. Besides, notes probably wouldn't have helped all that much."

"You don't need to make excuses for me. Do you really believe," she demanded of him again, "after all that's happened and all that's been said, that he could still be alive after all? That I've been taken in by tricks and illusions, and that Mary also was deceived?"

"No, I don't. I don't believe that in the least. It would not make sense of all that has happened and in particular, it would not explain the death of Miller with his inexplicably frostbitten hands. I *do* fully believe you have met and spoken with someone who is dead.

182

Whether one chooses to call him a ghost or not is irrelevant. The terminology is not important. All I'm saying is that if you were to make it public, if you were to write an account of it, it would not be accepted as proof of anything. Your explanation of last resort would not be believed. In preference, most people would choose no explanation at all."

"I have no intention of making anything public."

"I'm pleased to hear it. Would you like another sherry?"

"I don't usually."

"The circumstances are exceptional."

"So they are. In that case, yes please, I would. You know," she went on as the vicar carefully poured two more glasses, "I can't imagine how I'm going to explain all this to Captain Kerry. He'd assume I was mad."

"You're still in touch with him, then?"

"I am, but it would be more accurate to put it the other way round. He is in touch with me."

The vicar handed Emily her glass and sat down again, peering at her through his lenses. "Is there any need to explain it to him at all? Could you not just neglect to mention it?"

Emily laughed. "I believe I told you before that he is a very persistent young man. However, you're right; not saying anything about it would be the wisest thing. No matter what I said, he wouldn't be convinced. He is too determined a sceptic."

"I've had a similar experience with some devout atheists, if I may use such a contradiction in terms. People whose beliefs are deeply rooted tend to be impervious to argument. They know they are right."

"You're not like that, are you? One would imagine a clergyman must, in the nature of his vocation, believe that he is right."

The vicar smiled. "There is a difference between *believing* you are right and *knowing* you are right. I try to maintain my position on the more modest side of that

183

demarcation line. I may occasionally claim definitive knowledge in the academic sphere, but never in the spiritual. That would be far too presumptuous of me. However, we are rather straying from the point about your captain. Why should you feel the need to tell him anything?"

"He's been very helpful. I feel under some obligation to be honest with him."

"That's most conscientious of you. It's not all though, is it?"

Emily hesitated. She was accustomed by now to the Reverend Small's knack of detecting nuances of motivation from her voice and behaviour, but it still sometimes made her uncomfortable. "Not quite all," she confessed. "It's ridiculous, but Captain Kerry has started to exhibit some unexpected... I don't know quite what to call them. Romantic inclinations, I suppose. Something of the sort."

"Why should that be ridiculous?"

"Because I'm far too old and plain for him. I told him so in no uncertain terms."

"What was his response?"

"He took no notice whatsoever."

"In which case, one must assume he doesn't agree with you. What makes you so sure that you are right and he is wrong?"

Emily thought about it, trying to find words for something she had taken for granted. "I don't know; convention, perhaps. The handsome young officer and the middle-aged spinster... it's all rather inappropriate, isn't it? A lot of people would find it laughable or what is even worse, pitiable."

"Poppycock!" For the first time since she had met him, the vicar seemed genuinely angry. Unfortunately, the only result was to make him appear faintly comic. His long face with the receding hair and wire-framed spectacles was not constructed for expressing anything so primitive as anger; it was too innately gentle and calm.

He made to put down his pipe, then changed his mind and poked its stem towards her belligerently. "Convention, of all things! I'd expect you to know better. I thought more of you than that. What does it matter what people think?"

"It does matter," said Emily defensively, "whether we like it or not. People's opinion makes a difference. One has to live in the world. Anyway," she added reluctantly, "that's not the only thing."

"I didn't think it was. Why, oh why, do I always have to press you so hard whenever anything personal is involved?" He had relaxed again and the pipe was back in his mouth. "You can be a most obstinate young woman."

"I'm not so young. That's the point, surely."

"To me, at my advanced age, forty is young."

"You're not *that* old. Did I ever tell you, by the way, that Mary described you to me as a 'decent old chap'?"

He laughed. "No, you didn't. But when you're nineteen, everyone is old. However, when one is my age, or your age, or even Captain Kerry's age, one should have gained some sense of perspective about these things. Tell me, have you ever encouraged Captain Kerry in his affections?"

"No, I haven't." She hesitated. "I suppose one could say that in some ways I haven't actively *dis*couraged him. After all, I do like the man and I enjoy his company. I did call him an idiot once," she added as an afterthought.

"That sounds remarkably like discouragement to me. Yet he persists nonetheless?"

"Yes. I told you, he's a very persistent man."

"Ah well." Small threw up his hands in a characteristic gesture, "there's no more I can say. You must make up your own mind on the subject of Captain Kerry. I can only beg you not to disappoint the captain

185

purely on the grounds that you feel you are somehow unworthy of him. That would be sheer selfishness."

"I don't feel any such thing," cried Emily indignantly.

"Good. For a moment I entertained the suspicion that you were feeling it without recognising it for what it was."

Emily glared at him. "No."

The vicar nodded placidly. "Good," he repeated. "Now, shall we return to Stephen Drake? Are you intending to take that matter any further?"

"No, I don't think so. In fact, I'm sure I'm not. It's over and, in my mind at least, an explanation has been provided."

"The explanation of last resort?"

"Yes. I never believed I'd hear myself say it, but yes. I accept that I will never be able to convince anyone else, that I have no true scientific evidence, but... I know what I saw, and heard, and felt. However, it's a sorry tale and it involves people I have known. I have no intention of making it public in any way."

"That is what I hoped you'd say. And if I may ask, does your explanation help you at all in your own private quest? Pardon me if that is an intrusive question."

Emily smiled. "You have a way of asking intrusive questions, however apologetically you may phrase them. The answer is no, it doesn't. I always assumed it would, that if ever I were to discover anything definite, anything positive, then I would know what my mother experienced. But in fact, it makes no difference. What I have seen may lend some small credence to the possibility that she saw something similar, though the two cases are actually quite different, but it certainly doesn't prove it. She may simply have been unhinged by grief. Nothing has changed."

"I can see that. It must be a bitter disappointment for you."

"It was all a long time ago. Perhaps I've made too much of it, allowed too much of my life to be influenced by it." She stood up. "But I must go now. As always, I have a train to catch."

"There's no need to disturb Mrs Claypole. I'll escort you to the door."

In the hallway, Emily paused to adjust her hat before facing the world, using a mirror hung there for that purpose. The familiar face stared back at her from beneath the brim of the hat, the fine lines at the corners of her eyes and around her mouth somehow more prominent than usual. Her face was pale; perhaps she had not yet totally recovered from her bout of influenza. Or perhaps, she ruefully admitted to herself, she was just growing older and searching for excuses. She noticed Small's face behind her, also studying the mirror and meeting her eyes in the reflection. She realised she had been regarding her own image for too long, inviting accusations of vanity though that was as far from the truth as anything could be.

"I believe I told you once that I had been married," he said irrelevantly.

"Yes, you did. Happily married, you said."

He nodded. "That's true, very happily. Did I also mention that my wife was somewhat older than myself and from a quite different social background?"

"No, you failed to mention that."

"I'm not surprised. I rarely mention it for the simple reason that neither of us ever considered it worth mentioning. Other people did, of course, sometimes maliciously. We ignored them as best we could. If I became a little impatient with you a few minutes ago, you now know why."

"I do. Thank you for telling me. You're a wise man, Mr Small."

He laughed and opened the door for her. "Oh no, I'd never claim that distinction. I hope we'll meet again,

Miss Duncan and that next time the circumstances will be less stressful."

"I hope so too." She stood in the doorway and looked up. "Do you think it will snow again?"

"I doubt it. That's not an example of my wisdom, by the way. I consulted the weather forecast earlier today."

Chapter XX

Emily stayed on in her hotel for several days. Her first intention had been to close the entire episode by packing and returning to London but several factors conspired to make her change her mind. For one thing she was tired, a condition she seemed to fall into more easily since her recent illness. Also, although the weather was still cold in that part of the country, the newspapers indicated that it was far worse as one travelled further east; the snow in some areas had been heavy and prolonged enough to disrupt the railway timetables and make travel generally inconvenient. In London there had been heavy rain, and London in the rain was always depressing to the spirits. All told, Emily surrendered to the temptation of inertia and stayed where she was. She would treat it as a rest, a kind of holiday.

There was, of course, one other factor that influenced her decision but that one she chose to ignore.

Not that one could really ignore Robert Kerry. His presence was too frequent and too diverting to be ignored. Emily saw him every day at some point, for walks or meals or any other excuse he could think of. She pointed this out to him, but he was completely unabashed.

"Naturally. I enjoy your company. If you find mine annoying, you can always say no."

Emily never did say no, though occasionally it occurred to her that she should. Then one day, Kerry turned up – unannounced, as he often did – to tell her he would be absent the following day.

"It will no doubt come as a relief to you. You can see someone else instead. I have to return to the hospital for a check-up on my leg and at the same time an assessment of my fitness for duty. Presumably if they discover the limb has spontaneously regrown, or I've sprouted another one, I'll be declared fit and probably also court-martialled for malingering. Otherwise, my army days will be numbered. Apparently I won't even have to show my face again, just wait for my papers to come through."

"Will you be pleased?"

"I certainly will. Out of uniform at last."

"Actually, the uniform suits you. You're perfectly fitted for the role of an officer and gentleman."

"Nonsense. Wait until you see me in a new civilian suit."

"Not one of those awful things the government provides for demobilised soldiers?"

"Absolutely not. I'll squander my savings on a decent one. Besides anything else, it will impress potential employers in future."

Emily studied him and pursed her lips. "As a matter of fact, I believe you'd look quite dashing in a blazer and flannels rather than a suit."

Kerry laughed. "Well, I'll trust your judgement. You're the clothes expert."

The day he was away stretched out unaccountably. Emily tried to think of other things, but annoyed herself by constantly wondering what was happening to him. Would there be some unexpected problem with his leg? He rarely mentioned it, but was occasionally obvious that the artificial replacement caused him some discomfort. Could there be an infection, an unexpected complication? She told herself repeatedly not to be silly, but self-administered advice is rarely effective.

When he turned up at her hotel the following afternoon, he looked more cheerful than she had ever seen him. He was also dressed in a navy blue blazer with a plain tie and a pair of pale grey flannel trousers. He stood in the hotel lounge, leaning on his stick and looking faintly embarrassed.

"I bought them this morning, to celebrate. Ready made of course, but quite a good fit. What do you think?"

What *did* she think? It was odd seeing him out of uniform, as disconcerting as if it were a change of personality instead of merely clothes. He was no longer Captain Kerry. Emily had no idea whether that was technically true. She suspected it wasn't, not until the bureaucracy had run its course, but that was how it felt. For the first time, she could genuinely think of him as Robert, not as a captain. What, she wondered briefly, would Stephen Drake have looked like out of uniform? But she quickly pushed that thought away. Stephen Drake was no longer any of her concern.

"You look splendid," she said warmly, then regarded him with her head on one side, considering. "The tie could be improved. Something more regimental, perhaps."

He shook his head firmly. "No, I draw the line at regimental. I don't want to be reminded of the army every time I look into a mirror."

"Then plain will have to do. Come and sit down, tell me what happened."

She often invited him to sit, hoping it would be easier on his leg. Up to now, he hadn't noticed but if he ever did he would resent it. Emily made a mental note not to do it so often in future.

"Nothing happened really." He lowered himself into a chair. "It was a formality. They asked me a few questions, took a look at the leg, then told me to go home and wait for my discharge. A waste of time to be honest, but one has to do these things."

"I'm very pleased for you."

"The thing is..." He obviously had something on his mind, but was unsure how to say it. "Well, nothing much happened at the hospital but on the way there a most extraordinary thing happened, most extraordinary."

"On the way?"

"Yes. As you know, the train from here to the hospital stops at Abbot's Sutton. You took the same train yourself, didn't you?"

"I did, yes." Emily was glad she was sitting down. She didn't know what he was about to say, but she knew it would not be welcome. She felt weak.

"Well, when it stopped I dropped the window for a glance outside. I don't know why, just wanted to have a look round. I was leaning out of the window, smoking, and at first I thought the platform was deserted. Then I saw there was someone there after all. There was a man standing on his own some distance away, a soldier in uniform."

"A soldier," Emily repeated automatically. She knew now at least a part of what was coming, knew it with a dreadful certainty.

"That's right. Nothing unusual about that, but the thing is, this man was the spitting image of Stephen Drake; exactly like him. In fact, if I hadn't known Drake was dead I'd have sworn it *was* him, that was how alike they were. Then, while I was watching him, the man grinned and waved at me as if he knew me. After that he remembered I was an officer and saluted. A damned sloppy salute it was too."

"Extraordinary, as you say," Emily agreed, trying to prevent her voice from shaking. She was remembering Drake at the graveside saying '*He's a decent sort, the captain, despite being an officer. I'd quite like to see him again myself, if it were possible.*'. It had been possible, after all.

"Quite, but that wasn't the end of it. As the train pulled out, the man took off his cap and just threw it away. Just like that, held it by the peak then sent it skimming through the air."

"He can't have!" exclaimed Emily involuntarily.

"Why not?"

192

Because he had left that cap on a grave several days before. But she hadn't told Robert about that, hadn't said anything about it. And Drake himself had said '*I was always leaving mine lying about... It always did turn up, of course. I expect it will again, unfortunately*'. So it had, but now perhaps it was thrown away for good. "No reason," she said, "it just sounds so unlikely, that's all."

"That's exactly what I thought. I was so surprised I watched the cap as it disappeared over the train, then when I looked back the fellow had disappeared; ducked into the waiting room or something I expect, while I was distracted. Anyway, he'd gone. Then the train pulled out. That's about it, really."

"You're right," Emily agreed with him. "It is quite extraordinary."

"Yes." Kerry sat playing with his walking stick, transferring it unnecessarily from hand to hand and avoiding her eye. He looked nervous. "To be frank, I wasn't sure whether to tell you about it. You haven't said much, but I've gathered you're reluctant to talk about the matter any more. You never mention it, which is noticeable because it's what brought us together in the first place. In the end, I decided I couldn't just say nothing."

As I said nothing about the graveside, Emily thought. Aloud, she said, "It's true I don't like to discuss it now. The two deaths, and especially Mary's, make it more than a disinterested investigation. After what you've been through, I expect you consider it squeamish of me to be so perturbed over just two deaths, but there it is. I'm not as used to violent death as you must be."

"You don't want to become used to it, believe me. I'm glad you're not and I hope you never will be."

"Don't worry about having told me, anyway. I'm pleased you did."

"I thought it might help. I mean, if there's someone around who so uncannily resembles Drake and who has a knack of vanishing when one's not looking, that may go some way to explaining Mary's experience, don't you think?"

"It doesn't explain everything."

"No. Not everything, obviously, but it may be a start..."

"You never considered," asked Emily, interrupting him, "that it may not have been someone who resembled Drake, but that it may have been Drake himself?"

He looked surprised. "Not at all. It couldn't have been him. Drake's dead. I saw him die."

"So you did." She stood up. "Let's not talk about it any more. I'd like to go for a walk. Would you care to accompany me?"

"There's nothing I'd like better."

The last word, thought Emily as they emerged from the hotel into the cold air, had already been spoken by the Reverend Small when he had told her ' *Your explanation of last resort would not be believed. In preference, most people would choose no explanation at all*'. He had been right, as ever.

Printed in Great Britain
by Amazon